Sabrina Turned,

watching him approach, her expression hidden by sunglasses.

Michael felt a sudden charge of energy run through him, like a bolt of electricity. Damned if he didn't suffer the same reaction every time he saw her: his mouth went dry, and his heartbeat seemed to triple.

There was something about the way she stood there, patiently waiting for him—the tilt of her head, the curve of her cheek, the soft wisps of hair fluttering around her face.

He had a sudden feeling of having experienced this same scene many times before: walking toward her, returning to her—always knowing that she was there waiting for him.

He wondered if he was losing his mind.

Dear Reader:

Welcome to Silhouette! What better way to celebrate St. Valentine's Day and all the romance that goes with it than to indulge yourself with a Silhouette Desire?

If this is your first Desire, let me extend an invitation for you to sit back, kick off your shoes and enjoy. If you are a regular reader, you already know what awaits you.

A Silhouette Desire can encompass many varying moods and tones. The books can be deeply emotional and dramatic, or charming and lighthearted. But no matter what, each and every one is a sensual, compelling love story written by and for today's women.

I know you'll enjoy February's *Man of the Month*, *A Loving Spirit* by Annette Broadrick. But I think *all* of the February books are terrific. Give in to Desire . . . you'll be glad you did!

All the best,

Lucia Macro
Senior Editor

ANNETTE BROADRICK
A LOVING SPIRIT

SILHOUETTE *Desire*

Published by Silhouette Books New York

America's Publisher of Contemporary Romance

SILHOUETTE BOOKS
300 East 42nd St., New York, N.Y. 10017

ISBN: 0-373-05552-8

First Silhouette Books printing February 1990

ANNETTE BROADRICK

lives on the shores of The Lake of the Ozarks in Missouri where she spends her time doing what she loves most—reading and writing romantic fiction. "For twenty-five years I lived in various large cities, working as a legal secretary, a very high-stress occupation. I never thought I was capable of making a career change at this point in my life, but thanks to Silhouette I am now able to write full-time in the peaceful surroundings that have turned my life into a dream come true."

To Michael,
wherever you are

Prologue

Jonathan had been nervous ever since he had received the summons to leave his duties and appear before Gabriel. Very few associates at Jonathan's level had ever been in Gabriel's presence. There was seldom a need for personal contact. Gabriel's communications were unfailingly clear and concise. Misunderstandings did not occur in Jonathan's dimension. That was not always the case on the earthly plane where he spent most of his time.

There were days when Jonathan became frustrated in his efforts to communicate with his charge. He had known that the position of official guide and protector to Sabrina Sheldon would not be easy, but it had certainly had its compensations.

Jonathan was besotted with Sabrina. And why not? He had been with her since shortly before her birth, thirty-six Earth years ago. He had joined her in order to prepare her for the traumatic occurrence known as birth. He had accepted the assignment with enthusiasm and pride, grateful for the faith his superiors had in him.

Now he shook his head, remembering some of the difficulties he'd had in his efforts to guide, protect and gently nudge Sabrina onto the paths that would ease her way through life. Jonathan had a hunch that his imminent meeting with Gabriel would bring to light some areas where improvement was needed. He grimaced at the thought. He wasn't looking forward to the meeting. Not at all.

"You wished to see me, sir?" he inquired.

In this dimension, time and space had no meaning. Therefore, his appearance before Gabriel was brought about by no more than the conscious thought that he needed to be there.

Brilliant light flooded the area, effectively shrouding the hallowed presence. Jonathan felt the loving energy emanating from his superior and began to relax.

"Yes, Jonathan. I've been going over the records on Sabrina Sheldon. I see that you have been assigned as her official companion throughout her life."

"Yes, sir."

"I also see that she has often disregarded your guidance and direction," offered Gabriel in a wry tone of voice.

Jonathan could not control his smile. "That's true, sir. She's quite headstrong. Likes to have her own way."

"I note that by disregarding your suggestions, she's created some rather traumatic episodes in her life, wouldn't you say?"

"Yes, sir. However, she has grown considerably as a result of those experiences," Jonathan pointed out. He tried to focus on the personage before him, but the shimmering light created such a glare that he was able to see little more than an outline of the man before him.

"Yes, I can see that," Gabriel responded.

"I've attempted to teach her the necessity for daily contemplation and reverie, sir, so that she would be more open to suggestions."

"Have you had much success?"

"Yes, sir, I think so . . . particularly now that she is older. Sabrina has accepted the consequences of her decisions and has matured quite nicely."

"But a marriage so young, Jonathan? Surely you could have persuaded her to wait."

Jonathan shook his head. "Oh, I tried, as did her parents. But she was determined to marry Danny Sheldon."

"I see she was a mother at eighteen and widowed at twenty."

"Yes, sir. However, she has done an excellent job with Jessica. In addition, she's built up a business of her own at the Lake of the Ozarks in Missouri. She has

a comfortable home, a wide circle of friends, financial security..."

"But outside of her relationship with her daughter, fine as it may be, I see no indication that Sabrina is learning about love."

Jonathan could find nothing to say. Both of them knew what the record stated.

"There's no mention of a man in her life."

Jonathan felt like hanging his head at that statement. Who knew better than he how little Sabrina had listened to his suggestion that she needed more balance in her present existence.

"Is there someone in particular that you feel would help her to discover the transforming power of love?" Gabriel finally asked when it became obvious that Jonathan was not going to respond.

"Yes, sir," Jonathan said with a sigh. "He was transferred to the lake almost three years ago, and I felt at the time that he was just what Sabrina needed in her life. He has all the qualities that suit him admirably to her, but..." He shrugged, unable to find the words to express his frustration.

"She wouldn't have anything to do with him?"

"Sabrina hasn't even met him."

"Who is he?"

"Michael Donovan. Sergeant Michael J. Donovan. He's been with the Missouri State Highway Patrol for almost twenty years. He's currently working in the drug-enforcement division."

There was a pause, and Jonathan realized that Gabriel was calling up the records on Michael Donovan.

"Hmmm. Interesting man," Gabriel finally said.

"Yes."

"I agree. He would be an excellent choice for her."

Jonathan sighed. "I know. The question is ... how do I convince her that she needs someone in her life? She shows no personal interest in anyone, even though she has a great many friends."

"What have you done to bring about a meeting between the two?"

"Sir?" Jonathan couldn't believe his ears. "What have I done? Well, nothing, sir. I have always been under the impression that we were not to interfere with that plane of existence." When Gabriel didn't respond, Jonathan went on, reciting the creed from memory. "We are to protect. We are to counsel. We are to guide. We are to instruct." He paused. "And we are never to take an active part in our chosen one's life. Otherwise their free choice is removed from them and their growth is hindered."

"I'm aware of the principles of conduct, Jonathan. I wrote them," was the ironic response. "However, a gentle nudge is never amiss."

"It isn't?"

"Surely you could arrange an accidental meeting, couldn't you?"

"I've tried. You wouldn't believe how often they've been at the post office at the same time, or the bank. They don't seem to be able to see each other, even

when they pass. Their homes are within a few miles of each other. They've even passed each other while boating, but other than a friendly wave to a fellow water enthusiast there has been no contact."

"Don't they have any mutual friends who might introduce them?"

"No one. They move in different circles and have no acquaintances in common. Believe me. I've searched for a link that would put them in touch with each other, but without success."

"Study the situation some more and see what can be done. Neither of them has much time left before their next test. Their chances of passing will be greatly enhanced if they have each other's support."

"I had hoped to get an extension for Sabrina, sir."

"I'm sorry, Jonathan. That won't be possible. But I have faith in you. Surely you will come up with a feasible plan that will bring these two people together. You've done a fine job thus far. I know you won't let her down now."

Jonathan felt a surge of warm, loving energy flow around him. He closed his eyes, savoring the experience, and when he opened them once more he discovered that he was alone, except for the soft shimmering light, which seemed to linger.

With a renewed sense of understanding of his mission and a sense of urgency about accomplishing it, Jonathan rejoined Sabrina, determined to do whatever was necessary to see that she learned more about love. Before it was too late.

One

I'd like to see some identification, please, ma'am,"
the large, shadowy figure told Sabrina, holding the
beam of a flashlight on an opened leather folder that
identified the speaker as Michael J. Donovan, a sergeant of the Missouri State Highway Patrol.

After hours of driving in the late-October rain-
storm, Sabrina decided that this had to be the logical
end to her less-than-perfect day. She'd finally arrived
back at her shop at one o'clock in the morning, only
to be cited for some unknown infraction of the traffic
laws.

Apart from his deep voice, she could tell very little
about Sergeant Michael Donovan. His wide-brimmed
hat protected his face from the rain, and a heavy rain-

coat shielded his tall body. She could only hope his mood hadn't been adversely affected by the lateness of the hour, the storm, and whatever it was she had unintentionally done.

She fumbled for her purse, praying that this wouldn't take long. "What did I do?" she asked, in as pleasant a voice as possible, handing him her driver's license.

He glanced at it briefly and asked, "May I have your permission to search your van, Ms. Sheldon?"

His unexpected request caught her totally off guard. Search her van? She must have misunderstood. Her attempted laugh sounded hollow, even to her.

"Is this some kind of joke, officer? If one of my friends put you up to this, I'm afraid I don't find it very amusing. It's late ... I'm tired ... I just want—"

Sabrina wouldn't have believed that his deep voice could drop even lower. "I'm on official business, Ms. Sheldon. It would save us both a great deal of time if you'd allow me to inspect the contents of your van."

What was going on? This couldn't really be happening, could it? She was not the kind of person the police would suspect of— Suspect of what?

"Are you arresting me for something?" she demanded, her voice shaking more than she would have liked.

"I would like to search your van," he repeated doggedly, praying she wouldn't demand that he show her a search warrant. He didn't have one, damn it, because he didn't have enough evidence to obtain it. All he had was an anonymous phone call and a report that included the fact that Sabrina Sheldon made trips on a regular basis between Hot Springs, Arkansas, and her shop in Osage Beach, Missouri. Such a routine could possibly be utilized to bring drugs into the area. He couldn't afford not to follow up on the nebulous lead.

"Well. I certainly have nothing to hide." After her initial shock, Sabrina was beginning to get angry.

"Then I'm sure this won't take long," he replied, for all the world as though she had just graciously given him her permission. She had no good reason to deny him permission, of course. She knew she wasn't doing anything wrong. But it was cold and rainy and she had no desire to stand outside and get soaked while he dug through all the boxes she'd brought north with her.

"Couldn't we do this another time? I'm going to unload this in the morning, and it would be much more convenient to look through them inside my shop." She nodded toward the back door of the Crystal Unicorn.

Michael knew that he would lose the admissibility of any evidence he might find if the contents of the van were inside the building. Unless he had a search warrant. He didn't have probable cause at this point, and he knew it.

"This won't take long," he said, striding around to the back of the van.

Thank God she'd worn a water-repellent coat, Sabrina thought to herself as she flung the door open and jumped lightly to the ground. The rain immediately drenched her ponytail, and water began to drip off the wispy ends that had come loose.

She stomped around to the back of the van, unlocked the door and threw it open. Crossing her arms, she said in a seething tone, "Go ahead, then. Let's get on with it."

Standing next to her, Michael realized that she only came up to his shoulder, but her suppressed anger seemed to make her taller.

"You don't have to stand out here in the rain, ma'am." He nodded toward the front of the van. "You can wait up there if you'd like."

"No, thank you," she replied in an icy voice. "I am just as eager as you to find whatever it is you're looking for that would cause you to be out here at this time of night and in this weather." Nodding her head regally, she motioned for him to begin.

Michael smothered a smile. Based on his years as an investigative officer and his ability to judge people, he would have been willing to bet that this woman had nothing to hide. But he couldn't take any chances. The drug traffic into the lake area was too serious for him not to follow every lead, no matter how slim.

He crawled into the small space in front of the door and efficiently began to unpack each and every carton. Every once in a while he would glance out into the rain, where she stood watching him. As the minutes passed and he found nothing that looked in the least suspicious, Michael's conscience began to eat away at him.

When he finished there was absolutely no sign of any contraband hidden away in the merchandise. Making sure that he had restored each item to its proper carton, he glanced around at the woman watching him from the open door.

"If you'll open your shop door I'll get these cartons inside for you." That was the least he could do for her.

"That won't be necessary."

Michael felt his frustration mount. Hell, he was just trying to be polite. Didn't she understand that tonight was the culmination of weeks of investigation that had led him exactly nowhere? There were times when he really hated his job with the drug-enforcement unit and longed for early retirement.

Tonight was one of those times.

Rather than argue with her, he lifted several of the cartons and started toward the door. Because of their lack of weight, he decided they must have been packaged for a smaller person to carry.

What a stubborn man, Sabrina thought, realizing that he was going to have all her merchandise as soaked as she was if she didn't open the door for him.

She ran ahead of him, unlocked the door and shoved it open. Then she flipped on the lights and pointed over to the far wall. "Just put them over there." She was ashamed that she couldn't force herself to be more gracious. She spun on her heel and went back outside. If she helped they would be through that much quicker.

On her third trip out to the van she dislodged a small box that had slipped between one of the larger boxes and the side of the van, knocking it to the wet ground. She groaned, recognizing the box, and hastily piled it on top of the others that she carried in.

As soon as she set the cartons down, she put the smaller box aside intending to put it in her car, which was parked beside the van. The contents of the box had nothing to do with the shop. She decided to let him bring in the rest of the contents and went in search of a towel to dry her hair with. She quickly untied her ponytail and briskly rubbed the moisture from her hair. The humidity caused it to curl in riotous confusion until she dragged a comb through it and ruthlessly tied it back once more. At least water was no longer dripping down her neck.

Picking up the small box that Rachel had given her, Sabrina walked back into the storeroom in time to see the highway patrolman place another load of cartons in the storage room. She could not see much of his face, because he still wore his hat. However, the added light confirmed her earlier impression. He was tall, with broad shoulders and long, muscular legs. She doubted that there were many people who would willingly tangle with this man.

She sighed. What difference did it make, anyway? They'd be through unloading in a few moments, and then she could go home. She felt as though she could sleep for a week.

Michael lowered a load of boxes to the floor, then straightened. The sight of Sabrina Sheldon standing there watching him stopped him in his tracks. Nothing in his investigation had warned him of her attractiveness. The vital statistics—red hair, green eyes, five feet eight inches tall—hadn't explained how that particular combination of hair and eye color, size and shape, could come together in such a beguiling fashion. Her eyes were shadowed with fatigue, but their green glitter threw sparks, and her hair seemed to catch fire under the fluorescent illumination.

Forcing his thoughts back to the job at hand, Michael nodded and strode past her into the cold, blustery night. When he returned with the last of the boxes he turned to her and asked, "Is this everything you brought back with you?"

"Yes." Then she looked down guiltily at the package she still held...the one that Rachel had given her.

"What is that?"

"Nothing that would interest you," she responded sharply. Sabrina could feel the warmth in her cheeks and lamented the fair skin that quickly betrayed her whenever she was embarrassed. "Just a gift a friend gave me."

He shrugged out of his raincoat and pulled off his hat. "May I see it, please?" he asked quietly, holding out his hand.

"No!" She put the box behind her and tilted her chin. Now that he'd removed his outer clothes, Sabrina saw the man clearly for the first time, rather than the officer of the law. She blinked, startled by her reaction to him.

She had already discovered that he was tall, but seeing him this close unnerved her. When she tilted her head back to meet his gaze she looked into his silver-gray eyes for the first time. His eyes were riveting, distinctive in his deeply tanned face. Thick black hair fell across his forehead, softening his face somewhat.

Michael couldn't decide whether this woman was one of the coolest smugglers he'd ever had reason to search or whether she was innocent, but for the first time since he'd approached her van she was showing signs that could be interpreted as evidence of guilt. He hadn't found anything large enough to contain drugs in the merchandise. Even the box she clutched in her hands might only lead him to search elsewhere. However, he had no choice at this point but to continue what he had begun. He had to know whether this woman was concealing evidence or whether she was as innocent as she appeared.

He held out his hand, uncomfortably aware of how her porcelain complexion glowed in the light. Michael had a sudden, totally inappropriate urge to brush his hand against her cheek, just to verify that her skin felt as soft as it looked. Jade-green eyes glared at him as her cheeks turned crimson. Out of guilt, perhaps. Michael was surprised to discover that he hoped he'd been wrong about this woman. He didn't want her to be involved in something as sordid as drug smuggling.

The silence seemed to beat all around them as they stood there facing each other, her with defiance, him with stubborn determination.

Finally Sabrina's shoulders drooped. "Oh, this is ridiculous! Here!" She handed him the package with a mixture of anger, embarrassment and disgust, watching helplessly as he lifted the lid and brushed the tissue paper aside.

A pale green nightgown lay nestled in the soft paper. Michael could feel the heat suffuse his face. No one could smuggle much of anything in something like this. Unconsciously he slid his fingers beneath the shimmering material, verifying how revealing it would be against her body. When he glanced up, he saw that her cheeks glowed even brighter than before.

"Very nice."

"I doubt that you've been taking up our time looking for something like that," she said. Her voice shook slightly... whether from anger or embarrassment, he didn't know.

"I apologize for any inconvenience I've caused you, Ms. Sheldon." He returned the box to her.

"Exactly what is it you thought you were going to find, Officer?"

"There's considerable trafficking in drugs here at the lake, Ms. Sheldon. Your periodic trips caught our attention. We felt we had enough reason to search you this trip."

"Drugs! You must be out of your mind. I'd have nothing to do with anything like that."

He nodded. "I'm pleased to hear that, ma'am." He almost smiled. Almost but not quite.

"How dare you search my van without a warrant of some kind."

"You gave me permission, remember?"

She hated his reasonable tone and his bland expression. She was so angry that she was shaking. How dare he treat her this way? He had no right. He had— "Do I need your permission to ask you to leave now?" she demanded.

He shook his head. "No, ma'am, you don't. Once again, I do apologize for any inconvenience I may have caused." He looked around at the cluttered storeroom, then picked up his brimmed hat and placed it on his head. Without another word, he pulled on his raincoat, nodded politely to her and disappeared into the stormy night.

Sabrina stood there in silence, watching the patrol car pull away. She could feel the tension leaving her body and the fatigue that had been lurking take over.

She couldn't remember the last time she had been so angry. How dare that man investigate her? How dare he treat her like some kind of a suspect?

And the way he had looked at the nightgown that Rachel had teasingly presented to her! She could have died of embarrassment. Did he think she actually slept in things like that? Rachel had embarrassed her enough with all her suggestions about improving her love life. Now this! Thank God she'd never see the man again. She'd never be able to face him.

Michael returned the patrol car to the station, climbed into his late-model truck and started home. While he drove, his mind continued to mull over his present investigation.

After the search and the limited contact with Sabrina Sheldon he would have been willing to place his twenty years' law enforcement experience on the line and say that she had nothing to do with the drug traffic in and around the lake.

He had dealt with a great many people involved in such activity, and he knew he could rely on his instincts. Sabrina Sheldon wasn't capable of the deception, the toughness and the cynicism that accompanied a life of illegal trafficking. Accepting that mental verdict seemed to take a load off his shoulders, and he knew he had to face the reason why.

He was attracted to the woman.

Damn. Who needed that complication in his life? Not him. Of course there had been women in his life over the past several years. He wasn't a monk, after all. But the relationships had been clearly defined from the beginning. He and his lovers had known what they expected from each other, and when the relationships had ended there had been no hard feelings or harsh regrets.

His instincts already told him that Sabrina was different. Perhaps he knew too much about her. Information gathered over the past few weeks had painted a picture of a solitary woman who appeared to be self-sufficient. At first he had interpreted her independence as toughness, but then he had seen her vulnerability, and it had called out to him for understanding and protection.

What the hell was the matter with him, anyway?

He pulled into the garage of his multilevel home overlooking the lake and turned off the ignition with a sigh. God, he was tired. Tired of the long hours, the unsatisfactory results, tired of his life-style. For some reason, that made him shift restlessly. He realized that he was tired of being alone. His restlessness stemmed from the encounter with Sabrina Sheldon.

What was she doing now? Probably still cursing him. Then she would go home, shower, maybe, or soak in a steaming tub of bubbles, then put on that filmy concoction he had seen . . . and touched . . . and imagined against her body.

Disgusted with his imagination and frustrated that he couldn't seem to keep her out of his mind, Michael got out of the truck and walked down the steps to his house.

His home was too large for one person, but he had known the moment the realtor had shown it to him that he had to have it. Because of his inheritance, he'd been able to afford it.

The main floor was open, with a cathedral ceiling that soared two stories. One wall was glass and revealed the ever-changing moods of the lake. A small kitchen was nestled in the corner, separated from the large expanse by an island-bar combination. Michael ate most of his meals at the bar, when he didn't carry them out to the redwood deck to better enjoy the peace and tranquillity of the water and the oak woods around him.

A massive stone fireplace covered most of the third wall, and the fourth wall supported the stairs to the loft bedroom where he slept.

He walked over to the refrigerator and stared at its contents. Nothing looked appetizing. He grabbed a bottle of beer, then closed the door. After he twisted off the cap, he took a long swallow, enjoying the sensation of the cool liquid coursing down his parched throat.

He stared out the window and watched as the rain continued to batter the glass that protected him from the elements. What a night.

He'd watched and waited for Sabrina Sheldon for over four hours, after putting in a ten-hour day. He shook his head. And for what? A chance to admire fragile glass figurines and a filmy nightgown.

He wandered over to the staircase and took the steps leading downward. Flipping on the light switch, he looked at the large game room located on the lower level and the green expanse of the pool table.

Maybe he would shoot some pool. It might help him to unwind. He picked up his cue and placed the balls in the triangular rack on the pool table. He knew he was too tired to sleep—too tired and too wired. He hadn't known what he would find or how she would react to the discovery of contraband. He never did. He'd learned to be prepared for any eventuality.

Failure to find anything had been a letdown, but it was one he was used to. Now he had to unwind and relax enough to sleep. He glanced at the wall clock. It was after two o'clock. No wonder he didn't have a social life. When would he have the time? Or the energy.

Phyllis's complaints had been valid. She'd hated his job—the long and irregular hours, his exhaustion, his lack of quality time with her and with Steve.

He leaned over and lined up a double shot, then watched as the two balls went unerringly to their pockets.

Steve.

Would he ever get over the ache in his chest whenever he thought of his son? When Phyllis had told him she was divorcing him he'd experienced the pain of losing his wife, but when she and Steve had moved to California he had been forced to face the loss of his son, as well.

Thinking about Steve would have him crying in his beer if he didn't watch it. Deliberately he returned his thoughts to the evening's events. Another lead had fizzled out. Granted, it hadn't been much of a lead, and he was glad that he hadn't found anything to connect Sabrina Sheldon with the nasty business of smuggling drugs. He would close the file tomorrow. But first he wanted a few hours of desperately needed sleep.

It took another two hours, three more beers and an uncounted number of games of one-sided pool before Michael managed to accomplish his goal.

Michael sat in his office the next morning, his feet propped on his desk, and gazed out the window.

The flatness he felt wasn't unusual. The anti-climactic feeling generally hit him at the end of an investigation, regardless of the outcome. What was unusual was the fact that he couldn't get his mind off the suspect. Or rather the ex-suspect. He'd fallen asleep the night before thinking about that damn nightgown—and how it had exactly matched the color of her eyes. He'd pictured her with her hair loose, falling onto her shoulders, the fiery tendrils contrasting with the soft green of the gown.

So he shouldn't be surprised that he'd dreamed about her. He found the impact she'd had on him downright irritating.

He caught a movement out of the corner of his eye and glanced around. Jim Payton, one of the men working with him in the drug-enforcement unit, stood in the doorway.

"Any luck last night?"

Michael shook his head. "Not a thing. She was clean."

Jim walked into the room, and sat down in the chair across the desk from Michael and placed a file on the desk. "Think someone tipped her off that you were watching for her?"

Michael leaned his head against the back of the chair and closed his eyes for a moment. "No," he finally replied. "No, I don't. She checks out as exactly what she represents herself to be—the owner of a small gift shop. There's no sign of unaccounted-for wealth. The call must have been somebody's idea of a joke. She even hinted as much last night." He rubbed his eyes, wishing he'd had more sleep.

"Alice goes into her shop every once in a while," Jim offered, referring to his wife. "Says she carries quality merchandise."

Michael nodded. "I can attest to that. I went through her entire shipment."

Jim fiddled with the file he'd placed on the desk. Michael knew he wanted to say something, but he seemed to be having trouble getting it out. Michael waited, feeling no need to pursue the topic of the moment and hoping Jim's thoughts had turned to something else.

They hadn't. "So what did you think about her?"

Michael lifted his brows slightly. "I just told you. She was clean."

"No, no. I don't mean professionally. Personally. Alice says she's quite an attractive woman."

Michael glanced out the window again. "So she is," he agreed, without looking at Jim.

"She's single."

Michael wondered if Jim would ever give up his matchmaking tendencies. Just because he had a happy marriage he seemed convinced that everyone needed to be married. Michael knew better.

"I'm well aware of her marital status," Michael drawled.

"You've given her a clean slate. So why don't you ask her out?"

Michael just shook his head. "You never give up, do you, Jim? I've lost count of the number of women you and Alice have dangled in front of my nose since I was transferred down here."

At least Jim had the grace to appear sheepish. "Alice worries about you, Mike."

Michael grinned. "Alice does, does she? I had no idea I held her interest to such a degree."

"You know what I mean. You're always spending your spare time working around kids. You should be raising some of your own instead of helping with everyone else's."

Michael dropped his feet to the floor and stood. He walked over and refilled his empty cup with coffee. "You're wrong, Jim. Dead wrong. I made a lousy father. I sure as hell wouldn't inflict myself on some other innocent youngster."

Jim heard the pain in Mike's voice and knew that he was pushing the limits of their friendship. But, damn, he found the man frustrating at times.

Donovan would let very few people get close to him. Oh, he was great working with groups, professionally or as a volunteer. But very few people ever got to know the real person.

He was one of the best investigative officers Jim had ever worked with, and Jim admired him tremendously. He just wished he wasn't so damned stubborn. But Jim knew when to back off.

Jim straightened the papers in the file in front of him and, without glancing around, said, "I was wondering if you would be able to help me on this case I'm working on? I have a couple of theories I'd like to run past you."

Michael returned to his chair and sat down, looking relaxed and at ease. Jim knew the look was deceptive. He eyed his friend uncertainly.

"Sure," Michael responded with a nod. "What have you got?"

Within minutes both men were absorbed in their work. Michael's personal life was not open to discussion.

Two

Sabrina didn't get to her shop until almost noon the next morning. Unfortunately, the extra hours in bed hadn't contributed much in the way of rest. As soon as she appeared in the doorway of the store her assistant, Pamela Preston, swooped down on her.

"Hi, boss lady. Boy, were you ever energetic yesterday! I never expected you to unload when you got home last night. What gives?"

Sabrina almost groaned aloud at the realization that the cause of her restless night was going to become a major part of her conversation today. She stalled for time, slipping off her jacket and carefully hanging it in the storeroom before she faced her inquisitive friend and employee.

"Actually, it wasn't my idea to unload the van at one o'clock in the morning," she admitted ruefully. She glanced around the shop, trying to decide where to begin with her various tasks and hoping against hope that Pam would let the subject drop.

She should have known better.

Pam cocked her head, looking for all the world like a curious bird, her black eyes bright with curiosity. "What happened?"

Sabrina straightened her shoulders into a quasi-military stance and said in a solemn voice, "The long arm of the law finally caught up with me." Then, throwing her arms out in a dramatic gesture, she exclaimed. "The secret's out. My smuggling days are over."

Pam's eyes seemed to enlarge with each word. "What? What are you talking about?"

Sabrina grinned and turned away, shrugging. "I'm still not certain that I understand, but somehow my bringing a vanload of merchandise from Arkansas seemed suspicious enough to the state highway patrol to warrant a search of all the contents of the van last night."

She disappeared into the back room and returned carrying an armload of individually boxed merchandise. Surely Pam had all the information she needed. Sabrina didn't want to talk about her last night's activities. She didn't want to think about them. All she wanted was to forget everything that had happened.

No such luck.

"You're kidding me."

Sabrina set the boxes down on the counter and began to carefully unwrap the contents. Without looking up, she muttered. "Why would I kid you about something like that?"

Pam hooted. "You? A smuggler? Don't make me laugh."

Sabrina glanced up and grinned, appreciating Pam's unswerving loyalty. "Thanks for the character reference. Who knows? I may need one yet."

Sabrina started back into the storeroom with Pam on her heels, firing questions. When she started her return trip, she paused and looked at Pam. Why had she thought that Pam would drop the subject before she had milked every possible ounce of gossip from the situation? Holding up her hands, she said with a chuckle, "Look, if you're going to dog my every step you could at least carry some of these in at the same time."

Sheepishly Pam scooped up a few of the small boxes and hurried into the display room. "Tell me everything that happened," she demanded.

Resigned, Sabrina recited the details that had haunted her dreams the night before.

"Did he find anything?" she asked when Sabrina finished.

Sabrina rested her hand on her hip. "Of course he found something—a bunch of glass and crystal figurines, wood carvings and folk art. He didn't seem particularly enamored with any of it, though. Maybe he isn't the artistic type." She continued unpacking and arranging the shelves, humming under her breath.

"Are those things illegal, do you suppose?"

Sabrina took a soft cloth and carefully wiped the lint from a tiny glass hummingbird. "If they were," she responded, making a face, "I would probably be in jail by now."

Pam unfolded and stored the empty boxes beneath the counter for use when the merchandise was sold. "Did he ever say what he was looking for?"

"Drugs."

"Drugs? You mean he thinks you might be involved in— Why, of all the nerve. Why would anyone think such a ridiculous thing?"

"Who knows? He said that the regular trips I make back and forth between here and Arkansas would give me the opportunity to smuggle drugs."

"I hope you told him what you thought about the idea."

"Don't worry, I did." Sabrina shook her head. "The most embarrassing part of the whole episode was his insistence on searching the box containing Rachel's gift to me." Sabrina still squirmed at the memory.

"Which was?"

"Rachel's idea of a joke. She presented me with a very provocative, very sheer nightgown, and Sergeant Donovan insisted on inspecting that particular piece of evidence very carefully, as well."

Pam's amused expression changed to surprise. "Did you say Donovan? As in Michael Donovan?"

There was something in Pam's voice that made Sabrina look up from what she was doing. "I don't remember. To be honest, I was so nervous I may not have gotten any of his name correctly. Why? Do you think you know him?"

"Was he tall, with black hair and a build that causes women to gnaw on their knuckles when he walks by and a smile to die for?"

Sabrina laughed. She certainly didn't recognize the description. "Well, he was tall," she replied, "but I never saw a smile of any kind."

Pam gazed thoughtfully out the large display window. "There can't be two Michael Donovans in this area. Now that I think about it, Tommy did say something about his coach being a policeman."

Sabrina knew that Tommy was Pam's youngest child. "His coach?"

"Little League. Tommy developed a strong case of hero-worship last summer. Mike Donovan is quite good with kids. I really enjoyed watching him work with them. He's patient and lavish with his praise and encouragement." Pam looked back at Sabrina with a mischievous grin. "You should have seen how the attendance at the games increased when he took over coaching—older sisters of the players, single mothers...he developed quite a following that never missed one of his team's games."

Sabrina concentrated on carefully placing the new items to their best advantage. When she didn't say anything, Pam prompted her with "So what did you think?"

Sounding preoccupied, Sabrina murmured, "About what?"

"About Mike! Isn't he gorgeous? Weren't you impressed?"

Sabrina took her time responding. She didn't want to admit what an impact the man had made on her. "I'd just like to know why he was so suspicious of me. Surely I'm not the only person around who travels on a regular basis."

Pam thought about the question for a moment, but she couldn't seem to find an answer, either. "Maybe it was just a routine check."

"No." Sabrina was certain about that, anyway. He had been waiting for her—had, in fact, followed her the last few miles to the shop, now that she thought about it.

Pam grinned. "Maybe it was an excuse to meet you."

"Very funny." She disappeared into the back room.

Pam followed her. "Well, what's so strange about that? Men are always trying to find excuses to see you, and you know it."

Sabrina just laughed, refusing to dignify Pam's remark with a response.

A lack of response had never stopped Pam before, and it didn't this time, either. "I just don't understand you, I really don't. You're involved with so many things, but you never take time out for yourself. Why, your personal life is practically nonexistent."

Sabrina handed her a stack of boxes, and Pam continued, undeterred. "You're young, and more than just attractive. You're—"

Sabrina brushed past her. "Perfectly content with my life, thank you, Pamela. I enjoy my life very much. I'm not looking for complications."

"I'll say. The most exciting thing that's happened to you lately was having Jessica's college roommate mistake you for Jessica's sister. You glowed for days!"

Sabrina chuckled at the dig. "You're right. I'm the first to admit that my life may appear dull to others. But I'm content. That's all that matters to me."

"I just hate to see you waste your entire life because of one man," Pam said vehemently.

The room echoed in silence.

The problem with having a close friend was that eventually you told them more than they needed to know about you, Sabrina decided. Then they had the audacity to use the information against you. For your own good, of course.

Pam plowed on. "I know you don't like talking about Danny, but face it, you've allowed him to mess up your entire life."

"What nonsense. Danny's been dead for sixteen years. I've certainly managed to put the past behind me after all this time."

They both carefully unwrapped glass figurines and set them on the counter.

"Except that you insist on keeping every man you meet in the friendship category. You won't even consider the possibility of another marriage," Pam pointed out.

Sabrina smiled, trying to hide her frustration at the turn the conversation had taken. "You probably haven't noticed, but there hasn't been a line of men queuing up at my door with proposals, either. None of that has anything to do with Danny, you know. We were just a couple of kids back then. I'm not the same person who fell in love with Danny."

Pam had heard that before. "Yes. I remember what you told me about him. He drew your attention because he was so different from all the other boys you'd dated. He was wild, exuberant, a maverick, a rebel—and you found him exciting."

Sabrina paused, gazing unseeingly before her. "He would have settled down eventually. I know he would have. We were both too young for the responsibilities of marriage."

Pam drummed her fingers on the counter. "Maybe so. But the point I'm making is that you've allowed one painful experience to keep you from trying again."

"I had a child to raise, that's all. I was a child myself, in many ways. I didn't have time for another relationship."

"Fine. So you should have won Mother of the Year eight years in a row or something. But what about now? You've been absolutely miserable since Jessica went off to college. You devoted your entire life to her. Now your life's empty."

Sabrina turned and looked at her assistant. Leaning her hip against the counter, she crossed her arms and asked, "Is this conversation supposed to be cheering me up? Because if it is, I must tell you that I managed to miss your uplifting message."

Pam chuckled. "All I'm saying is that your life doesn't have to be empty, boss lady. Now's the time to get involved with someone again. Learn to enjoy yourself."

"I do enjoy myself. I'm involved in all sorts of activities."

Pam gave an unladylike snort. "Business activities, you mean."

"Well, since I'm a businessperson, that makes a lot of sense to me."

"But what do you do for fun?"

"I've worked with the Lake Area Performing Arts Guild ever since I moved here. That certainly takes up any extra time I might have."

Pam just shook her head. "You don't see it, do you? You're so busy rushing around looking after everybody else that you don't do anything to look after you. You've carried the nurturing process to the whole blamed area. But who looks after you?"

"I don't need anyone to look after me. I'm just fine."

"Of course you are. And your acting abilities were never more evident than when Jessica called from college the other day. Real Oscar material, you are. You almost made me believe that having her away from home hadn't affected you much at all."

Sabrina could feel herself flushing. "I don't want her worrying about me. Of course there's going to be an adjustment at first, living alone after all these years. But I'm doing fine. Really I am."

Pam tilted her head and looked at her doubtfully. "If you say so."

Sabrina threw up her hands. "All right. I give in. The next time Sergeant Donovan decides to search my van I will insist that he invite me out on a date. How's that?"

Pam laughed. "Now that I would like to see."

Sabrina picked up some of the Styrofoam packing that was lying on the counter and threw it at Pam, causing her to duck. Pam finally allowed the subject to drop, for which Sabrina was profoundly grateful.

Later that evening, as she was getting ready for bed, Sabrina reluctantly recalled their conversation. She couldn't fault the logic of Pam's argument. She just didn't know how to explain to Pam that it was fear that kept her from forming any but the most casual of relationships with men. She felt uneasy, because she had so little experience in relating to a man. It was as though she had stopped developing socially when she was a teenager. As soon as she met a man she knew was single, she could feel herself tensing, becoming stiff and formal, unable to relax and chat as she did with her women friends.

She'd learned how to be a mother through trial and error, eventually becoming comfortable with the role. She felt too old now to learn how to relate to an adult male. Even the thought of attempting to socialize and date filled her with a horrible sense of inadequacy.

No. She was content with her safe life, she decided as she crawled into bed and turned off the light. She had lots of friends, and she felt safe socializing in groups. She saw no reason to make any changes in her life.

Lying there in the dark, she could secretly agree with Pam that Michael Donovan was extremely attractive, even when he was being stern and starkly professional. Surely he had missed his calling. With his dark good looks, Sergeant Donovan should have been on some television series—*Men in Blue* or something.

So what if she had found him attractive? She wouldn't have the foggiest idea how to relax around a man like that. She would end up a nervous wreck or—worse—she'd end up making a complete fool of herself.

As long as she was being honest with herself, Sabrina had to admit that perhaps Pam had a point about Danny, as well. She had loved him, and the pain that loving him had caused her had been more than she could cope with as a teenager. When he had died she had packed up all her feelings along with Danny's few belongings. She had returned most of his possessions to his family, except for a few things that she saved for Jessica. Her love she'd stored carefully away inside herself, afraid to offer it to anyone besides Jessica.

Sabrina turned on her side and curled into her pillow. Her present life was safe. She intended to keep it that way.

By Saturday Sabrina had distanced herself from the events of Sunday night. Following her weekly routine, she set out for the post office, the bank and the grocery store, wishing she hadn't overslept. Now she found herself rushing in order to make up some time.

As soon as she pulled into the post office parking lot she slipped out of her car and dashed to the entrance of the neat brick building. Just as she reached for the inner glass door, it moved away from her. Glancing up, she saw a pair of silver-glinting eyes in a darkly tanned face, thick black hair liberally sprinkled with gray and a frankly fascinating smile. White teeth flashed, and she heard the words "Good morning, Ms. Sheldon." It was as though they were coming from a great distance.

This dazzling specimen of manhood knew her? She quickly scanned downward, taking in the tan leather bomber jacket. the faded jeans that testified to the excellent physical condition of the wearer, down to a pair of scuffed but comfortable-looking boots. Numbly her gaze retraced its path, more slowly now, as though to make sure she hadn't missed anything vital.

The woman standing before Michael was a far cry from the pale and obviously tired female he had seen a few nights before, but he had no trouble recognizing her. None at all. He took his time inspecting her in the light of day. He definitely liked what he saw.

She wore a moss-green suede jacket and skirt, with matching pumps and a pale pink blouse peeking over the collar. Her hair was no longer tied back. Instead, it fell in waves around her face and onto her shoulders in a casual look that he found extremely enticing. Michael could almost feel his fingers twitching, eager to touch the fiery cascade of color...wondering if they would be singed... knowing it might be worth it.

When his gaze finally met hers, he was delighted to observe the heightened color in her cheeks. She was not unaware of him, either, if her flushed expression was any indication. Feeling more than a little over-heated himself, Michael was pleased to know that his reaction was not totally one-sided.

Somebody brushed against his shoulder with a murmured apology, and Michael realized that he was blocking the door to the post office. He stepped back, holding it wider and waving Sabrina through with a flourish.

She nodded a little uncertainly. "Thank you."

Sabrina took several steps toward her post office box before she realized who the man at the door was. She spun around, but he was nowhere in sight.

Michael Donovan! The highway patrolman! Pam had been right. He had a devastating smile, but that was just part of his attractiveness. She had found him appealing in his uniform, but the leather jacket he wore this morning emphasized his broad shoulders to a distracting degree. And those jeans! They should be outlawed in the name of decency.

However, it was the unexpected charm of his smile that lingered in her mind, causing her to fumble for her box key and drop several pieces of mail as she emptied her mailbox. Sabrina shook her head, trying to clear it. His potent smile dazzled and distracted her, making her feel like some easily impressed adolescent.

How out of character it was for her to act this way. Jessica was the one who noticed and pointed out good-looking men.

When Sabrina returned to her car, she was astounded to note that her hands were trembling slightly. What in the world was wrong with her? Hadn't she ever seen a handsome man before? One who spoke to her, calling her by name in a deep, velvety voice? One who smiled at her as though he found her the most attractive woman in his life?

Come to think of it . . . no, she hadn't. And she was more than a little uncomfortable with the turmoil that their recent encounter had produced inside her. She was no giggling teenager who was routinely infatuated. She was a mature woman, with a grown daughter. Was she going to allow her irrational reaction to a strange man throw her? Of course she wasn't. She had just been a little on edge lately, that was all. Maybe a little more emotional than usual.

Feeling somewhat more calm after the lecture she had given herself, Sabrina backed out of the parking lot and continued her errands. She turned in at the bank and pulled into a parking space next to a late-model pickup truck. As she started toward the door, Sabrina began to search for her checkbook in the depths of her purse; she didn't see the man coming out of the bank until she ran into him.

The impact was strong enough that she would have fallen if his quick thinking hadn't saved her. He grabbed her shoulders and steadied her, but her open purse went flying, strewing its personal contents along the sidewalk and in the grass.

Sabrina felt jarred by the impact against a leather-clad chest, and what little breath she managed to save escaped her when she glanced up into the laughing face of the man who held her in his arms.

Thoughts of apologizing for not having seen him flew out of her head when she recognized the man who held her. She had never felt so flustered in her life. Thoroughly rattled, she was mortified to hear herself blurt out. "Are you by any chance following me?" Without waiting for a response to her ridiculous question, Sabrina pulled away from him and knelt to pick up the scattered contents of her purse.

Michael obligingly knelt down beside her and handed her a set of keys, a lipstick, a comb and a half-eaten candy bar. Although he had carefully removed the smile from his lips, his eyes danced with amusement.

"How could I be following you, Ms. Sheldon? I was at the post office and the bank first. If anyone is following someone—" He paused, handing her a ticket stub, two grocery receipts, a compact and a tiny perfume atomizer, tactfully not finishing his sentence.

Sabrina had a fleeting thought about an unjust universe that did not allow a person to dematerialize on demand. She even considered the advantages of fainting or dropping dead. However, she had to admit that facing the humiliation of explaining her asinine comment was preferable to meeting her Maker at this stage of her life.

Or so she tried to convince herself.

"I'm sorry," she muttered. "That was a stupid thing to say, I wasn't looking where I was going, and—"

He waited, but when she didn't go any further with her explanation he asked, in a voice that seemed to affect her in ways she couldn't begin to understand at the moment. "Are you hurt?"

She pushed her hair out of her eyes, wishing she had taken the time to pin it up this morning, and looked over at him. They were still kneeling facing each other, only inches apart. She could see herself reflected in his clear silver-gray eyes. Absently placing her retrieved items into her purse, she could only continue to stare into his eyes and shake her head, unable to find her voice.

"That's good," he said, coming to his feet and lifting her, as well. He glanced around as though aware for the first time where they were. "Say, why don't we go across the street and have a cup of coffee? We seem to be on the same schedule today anyway." The smile he gave her almost caused her knees to buckle. "It would probably be safer for everyone concerned if we went together."

Sabrina panicked at the thought of spending any more time with this man. There was no telling what she might blurt out in her rattled condition.

"Oh, no, I can't," she replied, shaking her head vigorously. "I'm sorry, uh, really, but, you see, I'm already running late. I still have to go to the grocery store, and—'' She paused as she caught a subtle change of expression on his face. An uncomfortable suspicion about the possible reason for this change caused her to sigh and ask, ''I suppose you're going to the grocery store next, right?''

He nodded, trying hard not to smile. She could tell that he was having a difficult time, but she strove to ignore the grin that threatened to overtake him. She glanced up the street to the modern supermarket that had been built at the lake two years before. ''Over there?'' She was beginning to feel resigned. He nodded once again, chewing on his bottom lip, which kept insisting on curling upward into a smile.

She glanced at the bank, then back at him. ''Look, I'll probably be in here for several minutes. That should give you plenty of time to get across the street and park. I promise not to pick the same aisle as you, okay?'' She smiled brightly, secretly wishing that the man would refrain from looking at her as though she were a lovable but slightly backward child.

''What's wrong with a cup of coffee?'' he asked patiently. ''It wouldn't take that long or make such a difference in your plans for the day, would it?''

''I really can't—'' she stammered. ''I'm running so far behind already, and Pam—uh, that's my assistant—well, she's, uh, expecting me to relieve her, and—'' Why was she blithering on like this? Her brain seemed to have melted into a blob of inert material.

His expression changed, and once again she was looking at the polite, aloof police officer she had first met. With a distinct pang, Sabrina realized that she missed the teasing, warm and very charismatic man whose smile had affected her so strongly. Too late she recognized that her cowardly behavior was depriving her of an opportunity to get to know this intriguing man. No doubt she would regret her behavior even more at a later date, but at the moment she just had an overwhelming desire to escape. She forced her stiff lips into the semblance of a smile. "Thanks, anyway," she managed to get out before she spun around and headed toward the bank and safety of sorts.

Michael watched her disappear inside before he turned toward his truck. Well, she couldn't make it any clearer than that. He knew his approach was less than polished, but she had acted almost afraid of him.

Perhaps it was just as well. Since he had met her the other night, Sabrina Sheldon had managed to become something of a distraction in his life. Now that he had a flesh-and-blood person to go with all the data he'd turned up during his investigation, he found himself unable to concentrate on anything else for very long. He'd be thinking about a problem at work and remember a piece of information he had learned about her.

He would lie in bed at night thinking about her. He felt as though he could almost drown in the green depths of her eyes, go up in flames from fiery contact with her hair, and now that he had come into brief contact with her body he knew that having her in his arms could easily turn him into a stammering schoolboy.

Michael climbed into the cab of his truck. He knew he should be grateful for her lack of interest in him. The emotions she had already stirred in him could create a turmoil in his life that he didn't need.

Let's face it, Donovan. The lady made her intentions clear. She isn't interested.

He pulled onto the highway and headed toward the grocery store. Despite that morning's encounters, there was no reason to think they would ever see each other again. Michael tried hard to convince himself that this was no big loss in his life. No doubt sooner or later he would believe it.

Three

─────

I just don't understand it. I thought that once they met, felt the obvious attraction, saw how perfectly they suit each other, my work would be done. I thought nature would take its course. I thought—"

"Jonathan, old boy. You're talking to yourself. Not a good sign, you know."

"Oh, hello, Harry."

"Something bothering you?"

"I'm obviously not the person to be doing my present job. I don't know anything about matchmaking."

"That's no problem, is it? There are always seminars going on around here on any subject. Why don't you sign up for one on matchmaking?"

"I don't think even that would help me at this point."

"What seems to be the problem?"

"Sabrina shows no interest in forming a relationship, and a relationship is exactly what she needs in her life right now. In fact, it's imperative. I managed to have her meet a man who would be perfect for her, if she would just allow herself the chance to get to know him."

"And what happened?"

"Nothing! Not a thing. They keep walking away from every encounter with no intention of seeing each other again. I just don't understand human beings."

"Well, chemistry is a funny thing, Jonathan. It's hard to predict."

"But according to all my data their chemistry is exactly as it should be. She's just refusing to deal with what her sensory perceptions are telling her. She's going to ignore the whole situation!"

"How did he respond to her?"

"The way a well-adjusted red-blooded male would respond to an attractive female. He was already fantasizing about taking her to bed!"

"Well, I suppose that's a start."

"Not really. Well-adjusted males do that all the time, I understand. Doesn't necessarily mean a thing."

"So now what are you going to do?"

"I don't know. I just don't know."

"What does his guide say about the matter?"

Jonathan felt the jolt of surprise hit him. "But of course! I never thought about contacting Michael's protector. Thank you, Harry. You've been a real help!"

Harry looked at his friend in amusement. "Don't mention it."

But Jonathan didn't hear him. He was already looking for Michael's guide.

"Excuse me, I understand that you're known as Daniel and that you've been working with Michael Donovan."

"That's right."

"I was hoping that we could work on a little project together."

"Project?"

"Yes. I'm Sabrina Sheldon's guide."

"I see."

"I've been trying to get Michael and Sabrina together."

"Yes, I've noticed."

"But I haven't been having too much luck."

"Michael's been alone for several years now. I've done what I could to get him interested in a more balanced existence, but he's never responded to my suggestions," Daniel pointed out.

Jonathan sighed. "Another stubborn one. And I thought they would be so good for each other."

"Yes. I must admit that I was encouraged by Michael's interest in Sabrina. Unfortunately, she's giving him no encouragement."

"I know," groaned Jonathan. "It's enough to make me wish for another assignment at times." He glanced at his companion. "Only kidding," he added quickly. "Do you suppose that if we worked together we might be successful in bringing these two together?"

"Perhaps. It would certainly be worth a try. What do you have in mind?"

"That's the problem. I've exhausted most of my ideas. I was hoping you'd have one or two we could use."

Daniel was quiet for some time. "We need to make sure that they keep running into each other." He smiled. "I don't necessarily mean literally, of course."

"I suppose, but I'm beginning to think that continuing to have them see each other in passing isn't going to further their relationship much."

"Perhaps he could do something that would make her grateful to him, that would be a great first step, don't you think?" Daniel asked.

"At this point, I'm afraid to hazard a guess. If they would just relax and get acquainted I know that they would eventually recognize how much they have in common."

"Michael's so used to being alone that I'm not sure he's going to risk being rejected again. It's a very painful experience, you know," Daniel pointed out.

"Yes. Sabrina went through some traumatic rejection, too."

"It makes them afraid to try again."

"Yes."

"But perhaps if both of us keep nudging them to- ward each other they will give a relationship a chance," Daniel offered. *"With both of us working on the project, I'm certain we'll be able to come up with a solution."*

"I hope so. I sincerely hope so. I'm getting close to being discouraged with the whole idea."

"We can do it. I'm sure of it."

Jonathan felt a little better, knowing that he would have some assistance. With renewed enthusiasm, he returned to Sabrina.

Sunday morning Sabrina came awake with a start, then lay staring at the ceiling in dismay. What had she been dreaming about that still seemed to be affecting her?

A pair of silver-gray eyes filled her inner vision with their steady gaze. Thick black hair tipped with gray beckoned to her, as though coaxing her fingers to thread themselves through it, to luxuriate in the tac- tile sensations of silky strands curling around them.

What was the matter with her? She had dreamed some stupid dream that she couldn't shake, that was all. During the past several months her sleep had been disturbed more than once by dreams that had quickly faded as soon as she awakened.

Glancing at the clock, Sabrina discovered that she had slept past ten, and she was on her feet before she remembered that today was Sunday. The shop was closed today. She sank down on the side of the bed and closed her eyes. That damn dream had unnerved her. It had seemed so real, the man so familiar.

What man? Who would she be dreaming of, who would she be so intimately, so passionately, so— Her eyes flew open. Oh, no! She had dreamed about *him*! She refused to think his name, as though he would then seem less real to her.

So why would she dream such an embarrassingly erotic dream about a man she had barely spoken to during two rather brief encounters?

"Whose fault is that, may I ask? You never gave the man a chance!"

"A chance! What do you mean, a chance? A chance to do what?" Sabrina wasn't aware that she spoke out loud.

"A chance to get acquainted. If you would relax and allow yourself to get to know him, you might discover the two of you have a great deal in common."

"Says who?"

"Says me!"

"But you're just my imagination, and I refuse to debate the issue with you."

"!?"

She continued bickering with Jonathan while she showered.

"It's Sunday. Why don't you treat yourself to brunch at one of the local restaurants?"

Sabrina paused in the midst of reaching for the coffee canister. Now where had that idea come from? She rarely went out to eat—especially on a Sunday.

Now that she thought about it, however, she found the idea appealing. Jessica was no longer home, and there was no reason to continue to follow their old routine.

Pam was right. She needed to get out more. She needed to enjoy life. Have some fun. A quiet Sunday brunch might be a tame beginning, but it *was* a beginning.

With a newfound determination, Sabrina returned upstairs to dress. When she stepped in front of the mirror, she was surprised to see a smile of anticipation on her face.

Her smile was conspicuously absent a short while later, when she was only a few miles from home, following the winding lake road that led to the main highway.

Sabrina had no idea where the deer came from. Perhaps she had been paying more attention to the passing scenery than to the familiar drive. Whatever the reason, the consequences were startling. As soon as she saw the large buck standing in the center of the roadway, she twisted the steering wheel sharply and slammed on her brakes. No doubt as startled by her sudden appearance as she was by his, the deer spun away, bounding neatly into the surrounding woods.

Headed in the other direction, the car finally came to a shuddering stop after plunging down a shallow embankment and delicately resting its front bumper against a slender sapling. Sabrina rested her head against the steering wheel, somewhat dazed by how quickly everything had happened.

When Michael came along and saw the car in the ditch, he automatically slowed down to offer his assistance. He was on his way home after having picked up the Sunday paper.

He pulled up and parked across the road from the car, trying to remember where he had seen it before. Nothing came to mind until Sabrina raised her head from the steering wheel and turned to look at whoever was approaching her car.

Michael felt as though he'd been slammed in the chest with a fist when he saw her pale face with its strained expression. Sabrina! He ran across the remainder of the way and tore open the door of her car.

Crouching in the doorway, he asked, "What happened? Are you hurt?" He reached out and ran his hand across her forehead and along her cheek in a light caress.

She fumbled for her seat belt. "I'm okay, I think," she mumbled, disgusted to hear her voice shaking. She swung her legs around to get out of the car and found Michael still blocking her way, although he had come to his feet.

"Are you sure you feel like moving? You may be injured and don't know it."

She smiled and slowly came to her feet. Since Michael hadn't moved, they were standing only a few inches apart. It felt very natural to both of them when he put his arms around her.

"I'm afraid the only injury is to my pride," she admitted. "I feel like such a fool."

"What happened?"

"When I came around the curve—" she nodded toward the road "—there was a deer standing in the middle of the road. Like a novice driver, I overreacted and jerked the wheel." She glanced around at the car. "I hope I didn't damage the car."

Michael didn't want to let go of her to find out what sort of damage might have occurred. The thought of what might have happened to her made his knees weak. Had she hit the deer, it could have been thrown into the windshield. In his years of working state highways he'd investigated his share of bad accidents involving animals that had wandered onto public roadways.

He ran his hand down the slight indentation of her spine. She wore a light jacket that he pushed aside impatiently so that his hands slid around her waist, across her silky blouse, until they met at her back. The smooth material assisted the glide of his fingers as he reassured himself that she was all right.

Sabrina suddenly recognized that she was perilously close to allowing her head to rest on his broad, sweatshirt-covered chest. She wavered, longing for the comfort. Then her dream suddenly flashed into her mind, and she remembered some of the rather explicit things she had done with this man...and to him! She almost flinched with embarrassment. Within hours after dreaming that frankly erotic dream, here she was throwing herself into his arms!

Sabrina stiffened, bringing her hands up to rest against his chest. What a mistake that was! She could feel the steady rhythm of his heart beating beneath the palm of her hand. Her other hand—without the slightest encouragement from her brain—smoothed the sweatshirt that covered the hard muscles of his chest. When she realized what she was doing, Sabrina jerked both hands away from him as though she had been scorched. That was exactly the way she felt.

Michael stepped back, devoutly wishing he hadn't worn such embarrassingly tight jeans. They did nothing to conceal his reaction to her. He turned away, hoping she hadn't noticed, and walked to the front of her car. Kneeling, he checked the undercarriage, then reluctantly returned to his feet, making sure the car concealed the lower half of his body.

"I don't see any damage. You may have picked up some tall grass and weeds. You probably weren't moving very fast."

"No, thank God." She looked around, only now recognizing that no other traffic had gone by. "I suppose I'd better see about getting out of here."

He heard the doubt in her voice and guessed that she didn't have much experience with off-road driving. "Would you like me to move it for you?"

He saw the quick look of relief on her face. "Thank you. I'd appreciate it." Sabrina stepped aside and allowed him to crawl behind the wheel of her car. The car seemed to shrink once he was inside, and she watched as he adjusted the seat to accommodate his longer legs.

Sabrina walked toward his truck to make sure she was out of his way. She watched him maneuver her car with a skill she envied until he had it out of the ditch. He parked it across the road from his truck, then got out, carrying her keys, and walked toward her. His boyish grin made her catch her breath. He looked so darned pleased with himself.

She held out her hand for the keys, but instead of handing them to her he asked. "Have you had lunch yet?"

She shook her head. "I haven't had breakfast, as far as that goes. I was going to the Lodge for Sunday brunch before I took my detour."

He glanced down at the keys, as though they might give him some vital information. When he raised his head she noticed the color in his tanned face had deepened, giving it a ruddy glow.

"Would you mind if I joined you? I, uh, really get tired of eating alone."

Although his tone couldn't have sounded more casual, Sabrina noticed that he seemed to be holding his breath, as if he were afraid of her answer.

She knew what she needed to say. There was no future in their seeing each other. Besides, she found him entirely too attractive. Her heart had already forgotten its normally steady beat, just at the thought of spending more time with him.

But how could she say no? Her eyes searched his, wondering if she could explain that she didn't know the first thing about dating. His steady gaze seemed to fill with light as he watched her, waiting, and she felt mesmerized by the glow.

"All right," she finally responded, her voice breaking between the two words. She hastily cleared her throat.

His pleasure at her positive response quickly covered his surprise. "Say, that's great! I'll follow you over there, okay?" He handed her the keys as though he were presenting her with a medal.

His enthusiasm flustered her. Ducking her head slightly, she walked to the car, hoping she didn't look as self-conscious as she felt.

Michael waited until she drove off before he got into the cab of his truck. Then he carefully turned around in the narrow roadway and followed her. Reaching over to the dashboard to adjust the volume of the radio, he discovered a slight tremor in his hand. My God, he couldn't remember the last time he'd been this nervous.

Sabrina Sheldon was going to have a meal with him, that was all. This was just a casual, accidental meeting. Look at him—dressed in old jeans and boots, wearing one of his oldest sweatshirts. She looked wonderful in her short jacket and tailored slacks. The trim fit of the pants had lovingly revealed the line of her curvaceous backside when she'd walked away from him.

He followed her toward town, pleased that he had thought up the idea of eating together. No matter what he tried to tell himself, he wanted this woman to be a part of his life. Michael was smiling to himself when he pulled into the parking lot behind her. After finding a parking space, he started toward Sabrina, who stood waiting for him near her car.

She turned her head, watching him approach, her expression hidden by sunglasses. Michael felt a sudden charge of energy run through him, like a bolt of electricity. Damned if he didn't seem to suffer the same reaction every time he saw her: his mouth went dry and his heartbeat seemed to triple.

There was something about the way she stood there, patiently waiting for him—the tilt of her head, the curve of her cheek, the soft wisps of hair fluttering around her face. He had a sudden feeling of having experienced this same scene many times before—walking toward her, returning to her, always knowing that she was there waiting for him. He wondered if he was losing his mind.

Sabrina waited for Michael to join her while she concentrated on hanging on to her composure. She wished she could understand her reaction to this particular man. Her heart and stomach seemed determined to change places with each other, and she was having difficulty taking a deep breath. What was it about Michael Donovan that created such an intense reaction within her?

Watching him cross the wide expanse of parking lot toward her, Sabrina thought of a sleek jungle cat padding soundlessly through its natural habitat—stalking its prey. She had a hunch he would be merciless in his quest. He was probably very good at what he did for a living.

He's probably very good at everything he does, her traitorous mind offered, just as he reached her side.

"I hope you're hungry," he said with a grin. "They serve a great buffet here." He guided her toward the front door of the restaurant by placing his hand lightly against the small of her back. "I seem to have worked up quite an appetite," he murmured in her ear as he opened the door for her.

Sabrina hoped he didn't expect a reply to that last remark, because her tongue had suddenly gone numb.

The restaurant was crowded, and they were asked to wait in line to be seated. She was aware of his presence close behind her and knew that if she were to lean slightly backward she would be resting against him.

A man coming out of the dining room with a group of people recognized Michael and waved, calling him by name. Michael acknowledged the greeting, and the deep sound of his voice reverberated through her body. She stared straight ahead, praying to be seated so that at least they would have the width of a table between them.

Another group of people entered, and the resulting jostling for room pushed Michael solidly against her. He chuckled, and she felt his breath against her ear.

With a nonchalance she envied, he placed his hands on each side of her waist, as though to balance them both.

Her prayers for a little more space were answered when the hostess appeared before them and led them to a small table near one of the large windows. Sabrina sat down with a quick sigh of relief. Then she looked up and realized that he was watching her intently.

She brushed her hand self-consciously across her cheek. "What's wrong?"

He shook his head and smiled. "Not a thing. I suppose I was just wondering why I've never seen you before this week, since we seem to lead a similar lifestyle."

"Maybe you have."

"I don't think so. I'm sure I would have remembered." His gaze seemed to wander over her features, as though memorizing each and every one.

The implied compliment did nothing to steady her nerves. She glanced around, searching for another topic. "Perhaps we should get in line at the buffet. What do you think?"

He looked over at the laden table and the line beside it. "I suppose you're right," Michael stood and held out his hand to her. The gesture was so natural that she took his hand before she realized what she was doing, then allowed him to lead her over to the line that had formed in front of the buffet.

"Do you come here often?" he asked.

"This is my first time."

"Oh, I stop in every once in a while. I get tired of my own cooking."

Sabrina found it hard to picture this man alone. He was entirely too attractive, too personable, too friendly, to be alone unless that was his choice.

They filled their plates in silence and returned to the table.

Michael obviously had not been exaggerating his hunger, Sabrina decided, watching him methodically clearing his plate. She began to relax slightly. His nonchalant attitude toward her helped. Obviously he saw nothing eventful about the two of them having a meal together. He had no way of knowing that she never did this sort of thing. He, on the other hand, probably had a very active social life.

After the waitress refilled their cups with coffee, Michael leaned back in his chair with a sigh of satisfaction and picked up his cup.

"Did you get enough to eat?" His smile flashed again, and she could feel her relaxed mood slipping away. Did he have any idea how attractive that boyish smile was?

"I ate enough to keep me going for a week," she replied. She searched nervously for an innocuous topic of conversation. "Have you lived at the lake very long, Sergeant Donovan?"

"Three years. And the name is Mike."

"Do you like it here?"

"Very much."

He looked amused, and she realized that her nervousness must be showing. He looked very relaxed and at ease as he sat there sipping on his coffee and watching her. When she didn't say anything else, he spoke.

"I understand you've lived here for several years."

"That's right. Five. How did you know?"

He shrugged, reminding himself that he wasn't supposed to know much about her. "Somebody may have mentioned it to me. Your shop is quite popular, from all reports."

"Yes, I'm thankful to say." She glanced down at her hands, clasped on the table before her. Her thoughts had completely deserted her.

"Sabrina?"

She glanced up quickly. "Yes?"

"Do I make you nervous?"

Her gaze darted to meet his. "Oh, no. Of course not. I mean, well... it's not you exactly. It's the situation. I'm not very good at this sort of thing."

His face reflected his confusion. "What sort of thing?"

She waved her hand in a gesture that encompassed him, the table, the room. "I don't do much socializing."

He grinned, relaxing once again. "Oh. Neither do I. Guess that makes two of us."

"I guess so." She couldn't think of anything else to say.

"What gave you the idea of starting a gift shop?" he asked.

"I received a small inheritance that I wanted to invest. Glass sculpture and crystal figurines have always fascinated me—I've been collecting them for years—so I decided to turn a hobby into a profession." She paused, thinking about that first year. She forgot her shyness and went on to explain, "I had met Rachel one time when I was visiting in the Hot Springs area. She's such a creative person, and when I first got the idea for the shop I contacted her and asked for her help in collecting items that might prove to be popular. She has a shop where several artists work, turning out the products that I sell."

"How do you spend your hours away from your shop?"

Sabrina smiled at the casual way he asked the question, so different from the intentness of his expression. "During the winter Jessica and I watched our fair share of movies and worked jigsaw puzzles. We spent summers around the water."

Michael knew who Jessica was because of his investigation, but he didn't want Sabrina knowing how much information he had accumulated about her. He knew she would be offended to learn how thoroughly he'd delved into her life. He was just thankful that he'd found nothing in her background to warrant continued investigation, because that would have effectively prevented him from spending his off-duty hours with her.

He already knew he wanted to spend as much time with her as she would allow. So he pretended ignorance.

"Jessica?"

"My daughter. She's a freshman at the University of Missouri in Columbia."

"You must miss her now that she's away," he said, watching her expressive face reveal her feelings. He reached over and touched her hand, which was resting on the table.

Sabrina heard the understanding in his voice, and a sense of comfort stole around her like a cloak.

"Yes, I do," she admitted in a sudden burst of honesty, not only to Michael but to herself. "Jessica's father died when she was two. I suppose it was only natural that I planned my life around her."

"But it makes life a little rough when they leave."

Sabrina heard pain in his voice and impulsively asked, "Do you have any children?"

He nodded. "A son, Steve. His mother and I were divorced when he was ten. I'm afraid it wasn't one of those friendly divorces you hear about. Phyllis hated my job and the long hours. She felt I wasn't a stable enough influence on Steve. As soon as the divorce was final, they moved to the West Coast to get away from my influence."

"How old is Steve now?"

"Twenty. He's enrolled at Stanford," Michael's voice showed no emotion whatsoever.

"Do you see much of him?"

"No. I've tried to arrange visits between us, but his schedule has always been heavy. Phyllis saw to that. I flew out a couple of times to see him when he was younger, but we were both ill at ease." He shrugged, as though he wanted to shift some burden he was carrying. "We talk on the phone occasionally, but that's about the only contact we've had in recent years."

Sabrina turned her hand, which was resting beneath his, so that her palm touched his. She slid her fingers between his and squeezed. "No wonder you can understand what I'm going through now."

His silver gaze met hers. He saw her concern and understanding reflected in her eyes and realized that he'd shared with her feelings that he'd managed to keep buried for years. Instead of being embarrassed, he felt a sense of relief. She was a parent. She knew how it felt to lose a child from your daily life, to wonder how they were doing, to know they had another life now, one that didn't include you.

He looked down at their clasped hands and felt encouraged. They had found a bond of sorts, an empathy. It was a start.

Determined to lighten the mood, Michael grinned and said, "I warned you, I'm not very good at social chitchat. At the rate I'm going, we'll both be crying in our coffee in a few minutes."

She laughed, just as he had hoped she would.

Michael casually lifted their clasped hands and took her hand between both of his. "There's this guy I work with—Jim Payton—who's always pushing me to meet friends of his wife, trying to get me to go out more."

"Can I ever relate to that! Pam, my assistant at the shop, is forever nagging at me about the same thing."

They smiled at each other in mutual understanding. Michael was pleased to note that Sabrina no longer seemed to be nervous with him. He felt as though he'd achieved a major breakthrough.

"What we need to do is to convince both of them that we are perfectly capable of taking care of ourselves."

"You have no idea how often I've tried to point that out," Sabrina responded.

"So what I was thinking was..." Michael took a deep breath and prayed he wouldn't reveal how important her response to what he was going to say was to him. "...maybe we could do each other a favor and spend some time together."

He felt her stiffen, and he almost groaned. She pulled her hand away and placed it in her lap. He caught a hint of wariness in her eyes when she asked, "What did you have in mind?"

Michael heard caution, but he also heard interest, and relief swept over him. "Oh, I thought we might get together for a meal once in a while...or a movie. Something along those lines." He was quiet for a moment, and then he grinned. "Take today, for example. I've got the day off, with nothing to do that can't be postponed. Maybe we could do something to enjoy the nice weather before it gets too cold to stay outside."

"I'm afraid I can't today," she replied with what Michael considered to be an encouraging reluctance. "UPS delivered a large shipment of merchandise from one of my suppliers yesterday. I'll probably spend the rest of the day unpacking at the shop."

"Could I help? It's the least I could do after the mess I left for you to clean up the other night."

Sabrina knew that if Michael came to the shop she wouldn't be able to concentrate enough to get anything done. The longer she was around him the more potent she found his charm. There was no mistaking the fact that he was showing definite interest in her. She certainly couldn't deny her attraction to him, either, and that scared her. What had happened to her safe little world? All of this was new territory.

He sat across from her, waiting for her response. She had to have some breathing room. She had to have some time to deal with what was happening to her.

She needed some space.

"That's very kind of you," she finally replied, "but I really don't think so..." Her voice faded when she saw the look in his eyes and realized that he wasn't going to give up.

She found his determination a little unnerving—and exhilarating. Never in the past sixteen years had Sabrina been so actively pursued. She knew that she needed to learn how to cope with her reactions whenever she was around him. Perhaps if she started with small doses of him she could build up to longer periods of time, sort of acquire an immunity to his charms.

He saw the hint of fear mixed with excitement and rapidly decided to back off, at least temporarily.

Deliberately leaning back in his chair, he smiled his most disarming smile. "Okay. I'll let you work to your heart's content this afternoon if you'll have dinner with me tomorrow evening."

He waited for her answer with no sign of impatience, and Sabrina faced the fact that she could not resist this man.

"Yes. I'd like to have dinner with you tomorrow night."

His grin lit up his face. "Great. Give me directions to your place. Then I'll go back home today and do the chores I was willing to postpone."

She drew him a map of the route to her home, then glanced at her watch. "I really need to go."

"So do I."

Neither one moved.

"I can't believe I'm doing this," she finally admitted with an embarrassed laugh. "It just isn't like me."

"Maybe it's time for you to do something different, something that's nothing like you."

"That's Pam's advice. She thinks I'm in a rut."

"It can happen."

She leaned forward and said, "I've never seen anything wrong with a rut, myself," she confided. "It may look boring to others, but I find it rather comforting."

"Safe?"

"Exactly!" she agreed, pleased that he understood.

"I'm not trying to take you away from your rut, you know. I'm just offering to share it with you from time to time."

"I think I'd like that," she managed to say.

"I *know* I would."

She couldn't hold his gaze. Pushing away from the table, she said, "I really must go."

He came to his feet at the same time and walked her to the lobby, where he paid the bill. Then he escorted her to her car. Opening the door for her, he leaned down and kissed her softly on the lips.

"Thank you for trusting me enough to see me again. I'll pick you up tomorrow night at seven."

Startled by the unexpected kiss, Sabrina could only stand and stare as he strode toward his truck, whistling.

She rested her fingers against her lips and watched as he drove away.

Four

The late-afternoon sun was almost setting behind the western hills when Michael decided to call it a day and go inside. He had raked and burned leaves and split firewood until the restlessness that had plagued him since brunch with Sabrina appeared to have been conquered.

The woman had a powerful effect upon him. Michael couldn't understand his reactions to her. He found her attractive and intelligent, but it was that slight hint of vulnerability that caught him so off guard, that made him want to wrap her securely in his arms, protect her from any possible harm, and never let her go.

"Let's face it, Donovan. You're hooked, and you might as well admit it." He couldn't remember the last time he'd so eagerly anticipated seeing someone again.

Michael heard the phone ringing when he opened the door. He hoped it wasn't an emergency at work. All he wanted at the moment was a hot shower and a cold beer, not necessarily in that order.

He grabbed the phone. "Donovan."

"Mike, this is Rusty."

Rusty was the dispatcher of their unit. "What's up, Russ?"

"Weren't you investigating a Sabrina Sheldon?"

Michael tensed. "What about her?"

"She was admitted to General Hospital a couple of hours ago. Looks like she may have had a falling-out with her cohorts."

"What are you talking about?"

"A shopper at the mall happened to glance into her shop window and saw that the place had been ransacked. She called the police, and they went over there. They found this woman lying unconscious in the storeroom, apparently from a blow to her head. She was identified as the owner, Sabrina Shel—"

Michael didn't wait to hear any more. He dropped the phone, grabbed his coat and sprinted for the door, his heart pounding.

What in the hell was going on? Who could have done this to her? His mind raced as he took the curves between his home and the hospital as fast as he dared.

Sabrina! What could have happened? He should have insisted on going to the shop with her. But he'd wanted to give her a little space. Hell. They had both needed a chance to come to terms with what was developing between them.

Now this.

Michael pulled up in front of the hospital, turned off the ignition and grabbed the keys, then ran to the front door.

"Where is Sabrina Sheldon?" he asked at the front desk.

As soon as he was given her room number, he raced down the hallway.

The door was closed, and he glanced at the nurses' station. There was no one there. He pushed the door, started in, then abruptly halted just inside the room.

She was alone, her head turned toward the wall. The almost silent *whoosh* of the door as it closed behind him was enough noise to cause her to turn her head.

The first thing he noticed was how pale she looked—except for her bruised and swollen cheek. She was surprised to see him. Her attempted smile wavered, and she blinked the moisture from her eyes.

"You manage to turn up, no matter where I am." Her voice sounded hoarse, and his heart lurched.

Michael returned her smile, his silent steps taking him to her side. The blinds at the window were closed, leaving the room in shadows. He reached for her hand, needing the contact, and held it between both of his.

"I came as soon as I heard." Seen up close, her bruise looked livid and painful, and Michael could feel the rage grow inside him, at the thought that someone had dared to harm her. "How's your head?"

"Not too bad. They've given me something for the pain. I feel like I'm floating about six inches off the bed."

He lifted her hand and kissed her fingertips. "I'm so sorry this had to happen to you, honey."

"It wasn't your fault."

"I should have been with you. I should have been watching the store. I should have—"

"Michael, you aren't my guardian angel, you know."

"Well, you definitely need one. I don't dare let you out of my sight."

She smiled. "It was kind of you to come see me."

"Is there anything I can do? Someone I could call? Your daughter, perhaps, or your assistant?"

Sabrina started to shake her head, then winced at the slight movement. "No. I don't want Jessica to worry. I've already talked to Pam. She and her family plan to go to the shop and straighten everything before tomorrow. Everyone's being so helpful." She brushed her hand across her eyes, but Michael had already seen the tears. He leaned over and kissed each eyelid, feeling the quiver of her moist lashes against his mouth.

"I don't know what's the matter with me. I'm not usually so weepy."

"You've had quite a shock. It's only natural to have a reaction." He eased down on the edge of the bed, and she turned on her side toward him. Pulling her knees up, she curled around him. He smoothed the wisps of hair on her cheek back behind her ear, then continued to stroke his hand over her hair and along her shoulder. She wore a cotton hospital gown, and he found it as appealing on her as satin or lace on anyone else.

He really had it bad.

"I've never had anything like this happen to me before," she murmured. "I had no idea how frightening it would be."

"Do you remember what happened?" He kept his voice low and soothing and continued to stroke her gently.

"I parked in back like I always do. When I got to my shop I discovered the door was slightly ajar. I hadn't seen Pam's car, but I decided that one of the family must have dropped her off."

He could feel the tension in her. He squeezed her hand slightly. She returned the pressure before continuing. "I called out, so that I wouldn't startle her, then stepped inside the storeroom. It was a shambles. Boxes and shipping material were scattered everywhere. Unpacking is messy, but the place looked like a tornado had swept through. I called Pam's name, because I heard movement in the other room. When I started into the showroom I saw—" she paused as though searching her memory "—I saw a movement or a shadow and started to turn my head."

When she didn't say any more, he prompted her. "And that's when you were hit?"

She took his hand and raised it to the side of her head. He felt a large lump there. "I think I must have hit my cheek when I fell."

"That's quite a knot you're sporting, lady."

"The doctor thinks I may have a slight concussion."

"I wouldn't be at all surprised."

Her eyes were filled with apprehension. "Why would anyone be ransacking my store? We don't ever keep money there overnight."

"Perhaps whoever was there didn't know that."

Sabrina's eyes revealed her pain and confusion, and it was all Michael could do to refrain from gathering her into his arms and holding her close. She met his gaze steadily for a moment before she asked, "Does this have something to do with your searching my shipment?"

"God, I hope not, but I have no way of knowing at this point." He moved his hand down her back, which was left bare by the hospital gown. She accepted his caress, and Michael could feel himself relaxing for the first time since Rusty had called. Whatever was happening between them seemed to be mutual.

"Why did you think I'd have something the police wanted? I've wanted to ask you, but I never quite dared before."

Her hesitant voice touched him and, without giving the gesture much thought, he leaned over and lightly touched his lips to her cheek, brushing them against the velvety softness before he answered her.

"I received an anonymous call one evening. I've thought about that call a great deal since then. I was told to watch you, and I assumed the warning came because you were doing something illegal. Now I'm wondering if I was to watch you in order to protect you."

Her lashes quivered slightly at his touch, but once again she didn't pull away. Instead, she pursued the topic. "You have no idea who called?"

He shook his head, feeling the frustration of having asked that question many times himself. "Not a clue. I couldn't even decide the caller's gender."

"How strange."

Michael saw her worried frown and wished he hadn't allowed her to continue discussing the subject. She didn't need to be focusing on the case at the moment. What she needed was to rest, to get better and to get out of here.

Deliberately this time, he leaned down and kissed her on her mouth. Once again he caught the subtle scent of her perfume. Now he felt the tender curve of her lips, which steadily enticed him as they shaped themselves to his mouth, and without further thought he increased the pressure, tasting and exploring her soft warmth, familiarizing himself with the pleasure of intimacy with her.

"Young man! I don't know how you managed to get in here. Our patient is not to have visitors. You are going to have to leave immediately!"

Michael jerked away from Sabrina. Their eyes met, and he saw in hers the flush of newly awakened desire, mixed with amusement. He grinned in response. He hadn't heard that tone of voice used on him since Miss Casey, his third-grade teacher, had caught him with his pet frog in the cigar box he'd used to store his pencils in school.

He stood and turned to face the nurse, who stood militantly just inside the door. "I'm sorry. I didn't mean to disturb Ms. Sheldon. I'm the, uh, one of the police officers working on this case, and I had a few questions I hoped she could answer."

The nurse's studied gaze took in his jeans and sweatshirt before she sniffed and said. "Well, the police have already been here and gotten their statement from her. What Ms. Sheldon needs is rest, not harassment!"

He almost smiled at the stern countenance of the woman who had appointed herself Sabrina's watchdog. "Of course, you're right, ma'am," he responded. Turning back to Sabrina, he said, "I'll be by to see you in the morning, honey. Try to get some rest." Ignoring the nurse's presence, he leaned over and brushed his lips against Sabrina's cheek. He noted the slight agitation of her breathing and knew that it matched his. Straightening, he nodded to the nurse and slipped out the door.

The nurse turned back to Sabrina. "He didn't look like any police officer I ever saw! Why, he wasn't even in uniform!"

"He had today off," Sabrina murmured, still dazed that he had come to see her, that he had touched her so lovingly, that he had kissed her with so much warmth.

The older woman studied her with a speculative gleam in her eye. "And was the kiss routine police procedure?" she asked archly.

Sabrina could feel the heat in her cheeks but didn't comment. She was trying to come to terms with what had happened and how she had reacted to his touch. Was it the medication, or the blow on her head, or had she just lost her mind? Something was strange. He had treated her as though they were lovers, and she had responded, feeling comforted and comfortable with him. She had never reacted to anyone like that before. What was happening to her?

After a moment of fussing with the pillow and the covers, the nurse patted Sabrina's hand. "There now, that should do you for a while. Just ring if you need anything."

When she was alone once again, Sabrina played over in her mind Mike's visit to her. He had been so upset, and not in the least professional. He'd acted as though he thought he was to protect her, to care for her.

Once again, like some star-struck schoolgirl, she found herself touching her lips where he had kissed her. She grinned at the thought. She felt like a young girl with a crush, and at the moment she didn't even care.

She knew that she was feeling vulnerable and alone right now, knew that the pain from the blow on her head contributed to her emotional state, but for a little while she had felt safe, protected and cared for. Sabrina couldn't remember the last time she had felt that way.

Turning in an attempt to get comfortable, she closed her eyes. She would see him again tomorrow. He had promised.

Michael stopped by the Osage Beach Police department to talk to the officer who had answered the call about Sabrina's shop. Tom Hastings was in his office filling out a report. Michael paused in the doorway. "Do you have any information you can give me on the assault on Sabrina Sheldon?"

Tom glanced up and nodded. "Come on in, Mike. I was told you were investigating her."

"Yes," Michael replied, taking a chair across the desk from him. "What do you have?"

"The place had been ransacked. I'm not sure whether they found what they were looking for or not. Ms. Sheldon was in no condition to tell us anything when we found her." Tom glanced down at the report he was working on. "Do you think she's involved in whatever is going on?" His gaze met Michael's.

Michael walked over to the window and stared out for a moment, then turned and looked at Tom with an unwavering gaze. "No, I don't. She checked out clean. I've talked with her a couple of times. I see no indication that she's involved in anything illegal."

"Then you've dropped your investigation?"

"Officially, but now that this new incident has occurred I intend to follow up until we can get to the bottom of what's going on around here."

Tom tapped his pencil on his desk in a sharp rhythm. "Have you considered that someone could be using her to transport drugs without her knowledge?"

Michael sat down again. "If they are, I didn't find a sign of it. And I went through everything carefully."

Tom leaned back in his chair and said, "We dusted the place for prints, but if these guys are pros they won't have left their calling cards."

Michael ran his hand through his hair. "What bothers me is that if the intruders didn't find what they were looking for they might be back."

"There's that possibility, all right."

Michael pursued his line of reasoning further. "Sabrina lives alone, in an isolated area of the lake. There's also the possibility that they might wait for her there."

"The problem for us, Mike, is that we don't have the manpower to give her protection."

"Yeah, I'm aware of that," Michael responded absently. They sat there in silence as Tom continued to fill out his report.

Michael finally nodded, as though he had made up his mind about something. "I have an idea that may give us some time."

"Which is?"

"While you're running down possible leads and my office is checking the local drug suspects, I'll find a safe place for Sabrina. Surely we can clear this up in a few days."

Tom grinned. "That's why I've always liked you, Mike. An incurable optimist."

"It's worth a try."

"You bet. Who knows? Maybe we'll get lucky."

As soon as he got home, Michael called his superior and filled him in on what had happened, then discussed his plan. When he hung up, Michael felt better, more in control of the situation. He hated to feel helpless. He needed to be doing something, taking an active part in what was happening.

He just hoped he could convince Sabrina to go along with his plan.

Sabrina came awake with a start and sat up, her heart pounding. The muted sounds of the hospital at night reached her through her closed door. When she realized where she was, she slowly relaxed.

Sinking back onto her pillow once again, she became conscious of the pain in her head. The doctor had confirmed that she had a mild concussion. She sincerely hoped she never found out what a severe one felt like.

From the faint light at the window it had to be close to dawn. She had spent two nights there. Hopefully the doctor would allow her to go home today. She could nurse a headache at home as well as she could here. Surely there was no reason to keep her.

Sabrina closed her eyes, hoping to find some relief from the dull ache echoing through her skull by sleeping for a while longer.

What had the doctor said? Something about her needing to rest. There was no chance that she would be running any races for the next several days. She would be more than content to rest and recuperate in the blessed peace and privacy of her own home.

If only she would stop having these nightmares of being pursued, of hands grabbing at her from the darkness. For the first time in her life, she was experiencing fear about living alone. She knew she was being silly, but fear wasn't rational.

If only she knew who had wrecked her shop, and why. What had they been searching for?

Pam had come to see her yesterday with the news that nothing appeared to be missing from the store. Whoever had attacked her had probably been searching for something valuable to steal.

A random coincidence? A burglary that she had just happened to interrupt? Surely it would not happen again.

Pam had cheered her with a couple of nightgowns to replace the hospital haute couture, together with a saucy bouquet of brightly colored flowers and a cluster of balloons with silly faces on them. Sabrina couldn't resist Pam's high spirits. She had been smiling at one of her witty comments when the door had opened and Mike had walked in, wearing his uniform.

Thank God she'd taken the opportunity before he'd arrived to change into one of the new gowns, brush her hair and apply a touch of color to her face.

As soon as Pam saw him, she jumped to her feet. "Hi! You probably don't remember me. I'm—"

Michael stepped forward and held out his hand. "Of course I remember you, Mrs. Preston," he said with an enchanting grin. "You're Tommy's mother. I didn't connect the Pam that Sabrina has mentioned with you." He shook her hand. "How's Tommy doing?"

Pam had looked startled when Mike casually mentioned having heard her name, and Sabrina knew that her assistant would be demanding some answers as soon as they were alone. Sabrina wasn't looking forward to the inquisition, but she knew it was inevitable.

Pam responded to Michael with a chuckle. "Oh, he's having a great time, as always. Still in sports, of course."

She sank back into her chair when Michael walked over to the other side of the bed and, as though it were the most natural thing in the world for him to do, picked up Sabrina's hand, lightly stroking the back of it with his thumb. "Is everything all right at the shop?" Although the question had undoubtedly been aimed at Pam, his gaze fell on Sabrina and his eyes darkened.

Pam blinked at the tension that seemed to spring up between the couple in front of her. She cleared her throat, and in a voice that was a little heartier than necessary, she said, "Oh, everything's fine. I was just explaining to Sabrina that one of my neighbors, Mrs. Moore, has agreed to help in the shop for a few days, until Sabrina feels up to returning to work."

The look on his face was causing all sorts of responses in Sabrina. "You're looking beautiful, as usual. How are you feeling?"

She could feel her face flame at the tone, as well as the words. He spoke as though they were alone, and with a sinking sensation Sabrina realized that he was not going to hide what was happening between them.

Whatever that was.

She didn't dare look at Pam and found it almost as difficult to meet Michael's heated gaze. His eyes were very expressive at the moment, and if she was interpreting their message correctly he was contemplating leaning down and kissing her.

He wouldn't dare! Oh, please, not in front of Pam.

Michael must have been able to read her silent message because his grin widened, even though he contented himself with stroking the palm of her hand with one of his fingers. She could feel her body tighten at the provocative message.

"Has the doctor mentioned when he thought you might be able to go home?"

Sabrina moistened her lips, only to find his gaze focused on her mouth. She found she could hardly speak. "Possibly tomorrow, he said...depending on how I'm feeling by then."

Pam spoke up. "I've been trying to convince her to come stay with us. Of course, with three kids in the house it isn't exactly restful, but you know you're welcome."

Sabrina smiled. Pam sounded almost as nervous as she felt. "I know. But I'll be fine at home. The doctor said I need to stay quiet. I can do that with no difficulty. I can rest, read a little. It will be a nice change of pace from my normal routine."

Pam leaned forward in her chair. "Oh! Sabrina, I meant to ask you, have you talked with Jessica yet?"

"No. I'll call her later today. I don't intend to tell her I'm in the hospital. She'd just worry, and there's no need." Sabrina was very conscious of Michael's presence, and of his disturbing touch. Pam's bright eyes had not missed anything since she had walked into the room. Sabrina felt totally out of her depth. She didn't know how to cope with the charged atmosphere. She closed her eyes briefly, wishing she knew what to do or say to defuse the situation.

Pam came to her rescue. She got to her feet and said, "Well, guess I'll go back to Mrs. Moore so she doesn't have to spend too much time alone on her first day." She patted Sabrina's free hand. "I'll give you a call later."

"Thanks, Pam. For everything."

Pam grinned. "That's what friends are for." She glanced at Michael, her eyes twinkling. "It was good to see you again, Mike."

"Same here. Tell Tommy hello for me."

"Oh, I will. He'll be delighted to know I saw you."

They were both silent after she left the room. Michael continued to hold her hand until Sabrina felt she could no longer ignore his gaze.

"You never did answer me," he said softly.

"About what?"

"About how you feel."

"It's hard to tell, really. The medication keeps me feeling dopey, but without much pain. When it wears off I'm more aware of the pain, but I can also think more clearly."

At the moment, she had a strong need to have a clear head. This particular man caused her to do and say all manner of unexpected things.

"I can't stay long," he said after a moment. "I just wanted to check in with you, make sure you weren't feeling any worse."

She rubbed her swollen cheek. "I think my vanity has been wounded more than anything else."

His fingertips grazed her cheek as delicately as the wings of a butterfly. "The swelling and discoloration will go down in a few days."

"I know. I'm really being a big baby about all of this."

He leaned down toward her, taking his time, until his mouth was only a few inches away from hers. "You're doing just fine, honey. Give yourself a little credit. You've gone through a traumatic experience. It will take you a few days to bounce back." The warmth and desire in his eyes were unmistakable from this distance, and she almost groaned aloud. Then he kissed her, and Sabrina felt as though she had come into contact with an electrical current that sent tingling charges racing throughout her body.

Even remembering his kiss now could set up the same sensation of a current causing her body to throb. If she hoped to get any more sleep this morning, she would have to think of something more restful than her unprecedented response to Michael Donovan.

She recognized that she was a long way from gaining control over her reactions when, hours later, he walked through the door, just as the nurse was helping her into a wheelchair to check her out of the hospital.

He wore jeans, a leather jacket and a black-and-red plaid wool shirt that put Sabrina in mind of lumber jacks and the north woods. He looked wonderful.

"Hi," she said with a smile, unable to hide her pleasure at seeing him again. "You almost missed me. They're letting me out of here this morning."

He leaned down and kissed her cheek as though the greeting were routine, smiled at the young nurse—who was not immune to his charm—and picked up the small case that Pam had brought her clothes in yesterday.

"I know. I've been in touch with your doctor. He said he was letting you leave on certain conditions."

She sighed. "Yes. I've heard them more than once, I can assure you." She glanced around the room, not unhappy to be leaving. "Pam said she'd be by to get me."

"I've talked to her, as well. I told her not to worry about you, that I would see that you were taken care of for the next few days."

Her gaze flew to his face, which wore a carefully guarded expression. "You?"

"Um-hmm. I'm taking you home with me."

Five

Sabrina sat across from Michael at a small table in his kitchen, wondering what she was doing there with him, sipping coffee and trying to understand how this man had been able to step into her life and take over so completely.

She knew her thought processes were not working at full power, and she forced herself to concentrate on his explanations.

"We aren't sure what caused the attack on you," he explained earnestly. "I don't want to take a chance that there is someone looking for you personally. Rather than raise anyone's suspicions, I decided to have you disappear for a few days, if you don't mind."

"Do you think the secrecy is necessary?"

"Yes, I do. I'd like to play this one as safe as possible." He gave her his most engaging smile, and she wondered if he knew how susceptible she was to it. "It won't be so bad, will it? I'll be at work much of the time, and you'll have plenty of opportunity to rest and relax." He touched her hand. "It will also give us a chance to become better acquainted." *That's exactly what I'm afraid of,* Sabrina thought. *Having dinner occasionally or seeing a movie together is a far cry from living together!*

"Why don't you let me show you around the place? It's not as though we'll be stumbling over each other while you're here."

He stood and held out his hand to her, and Sabrina found herself responding. Perhaps she was overreacting. It was probably the pain in her head that kept her from coming up with logical alternatives to his suggestion.

She managed not to stiffen when he placed his hand at her waist. He had a beautiful home with a panoramic view of the winding lake that had at one time been the Osage River. Sliding doors opened onto a redwood deck that held a table, a few comfortably padded chairs and a couple of chaise longues.

"The master bedroom is up there. It has its own bath." Michael pointed to the balcony overlooking the living area. "I thought you might enjoy staying up there, although you may stay wherever you wish. There's another bedroom on this floor that I use as an office, and two more downstairs that are separated by a bathroom.''

She nodded toward the balcony. "Isn't that your room?''

"Yes, but I don't spend much time there." He guided her downstairs, where she discovered a large game room. A pool table dominated the room. "When I'm too keyed up to sleep I come down here and shoot pool for hours. I'm afraid I might disturb you if you were down here, but of course it's up to you. I want you to be comfortable.''

She rubbed her forehead. "Are you sure you want to do this?''

He turned her so that she was facing him. "I'm very sure.''

"But what about my clothes? I only have the gowns that Pam brought me and what I'm wearing now.''

He led her back upstairs. "Why don't you take your pain medication and lie down for a while? When you wake up I'll run you over to your place and let you pack a few things.''

Lying down sounded like a terrific idea. She would think about all of this later. "All right.''

"Great." He led her up to the balcony. The view was spectacular. When he walked over and drew back the covers, she willingly sat down on the bed and slipped off her shoes. He leaned over and casually kissed her, straightened and, with a smile that she found oddly reassuring, said, "Rest. I promised the doctor I'd see that you took it easy.''

With that he turned away and disappeared down the stairs.

Sabrina stretched out on the bed and sighed. She wasn't sure about what was happening in her life at the moment. She would have to think about it later.

Downstairs Michael took a deep breath and quietly released it. So far, so good. He couldn't remember the last time he'd worked that hard to bring something to pass. Perhaps he'd been a little high-handed in picking her up and bringing her to his home without giving her a choice. Perhaps he was taking advantage of the circumstances a little. Perhaps, hell—he knew he was, but somehow he couldn't dredge up any feelings of guilt. None of what he had told her was a lie. He was worried about her, and he wanted to ensure that she was safe. If the bonus to having her safe was having her become a part of his daily life, he certainly couldn't complain about that. He just hoped she wouldn't insist on returning home.

Sabrina came awake three mornings later and was relieved to note that her head no longer ached. She lay in bed and thought about all that had happened in the few days she had been at Michael's.

Surprisingly enough, they had found a companionable routine, despite the fact that he was used to living alone and she hadn't lived around a male in years. Michael left early, long before Sabrina was awake. Sometimes he would not return until late at night. When he arrived home, she heard him, even if she had already gone to bed. Then she would join him, heat up his portion of the meal she had made earlier and chat with him about whatever he felt like discussing.

Sometimes she would sit and watch him shoot pool while he unwound from his day. What surprised Sabrina was how much she looked forward to sharing a few hours with him whenever he was there. Another surprise was discovering that she wasn't as anxious about not going to the shop as she had thought she would be. It was a relief to know that Pam would take care of things until Sabrina was ready to return.

She'd made her periodic call to Jessica, who had seemed to be enjoying school. For this little while Sabrina felt as though she had escaped her responsibilities and could do whatever she wished.

Michael had an eclectic collection of books, and she enjoyed reading them and discussing them with him. She'd also discovered that they had similar tastes in music. After being in his home for a few days she felt that she knew him better than friends she'd known for years.

She wondered if he ever slept. She would wake up some nights and hear the soft click of the balls on the pool table. There was comfort in knowing that he was there if she should need him, and she would drift back to sleep.

What she appreciated most was the fact that he had begun to share his thoughts, his feelings and some of his past with her. He told her about the pain he'd experienced as he'd watched his son grow more and more different from the ten-year-old who had moved away. He touched on the fights with his former wife about visitation rights and how he had backed off when he saw how much the situation was upsetting Steve.

She shared with him the horror of losing her brother in Vietnam when she was sixteen. He'd been three years older. They had been so close, and she had been devastated by the loss. Looking back, she sometimes wondered if losing her brother before he'd had a chance at life was the reason she had insisted on marrying Danny. Her parents had cautioned her to wait, but she had been afraid she would lose him if she waited. In the end she had discovered that he had never been hers to lose. But it had taken a great deal of maturity for her to understand that.

She told Michael so many things that she had never shared with anyone. The late-night chats took place in an atmosphere of intimacy created by the soft lights, Michael's weariness, her own sleepy sense that they were the only two people in the world who were awake—sharing secret parts of themselves, discovering how they had dealt with what had happened to them.

Somehow, in talking about the past, Sabrina found herself releasing much of the pain of the old hurts, recognizing that they were no longer a part of the person she was today. She felt lighter, somehow, as though she'd dropped unseen burdens that she'd carried for years.

Yes, there had been important revelations during the past few days, not the least of which was her discovery of growing feelings for Michael.

Sabrina heard a slight noise downstairs and remembered that Michael had told her this was his day off. He was home! She threw back the covers and hurried to take her shower, pleased to know he would be waiting when she got downstairs.

He was sitting at the kitchen bar, sipping a cup of coffee and gazing at the lake through the picture window, when she came into the kitchen.

"Good morning," she said with a smile, enjoying the sight of his freshly shaved face, the way his thick hair glistened in the sunlight and the warmth in his eyes when he looked around at her.

"As a matter of fact, I was thinking the very same thing," he replied.

She looked at him, confused.

"That it's an unusually good morning for this time of year," he explained. "I was wondering if you felt like taking a drive today. I have a feeling you might enjoy getting out of the house for a few hours."

She poured herself a cup of coffee and joined him at the bar. "That sounds like fun. Did you have any particular place in mind?"

"I thought we might go to Ha Ha Tonka." The state park was one of the most scenic spots around the Lake of the Ozarks.

He hoped she would agree, because he wasn't sure how much longer he was going to be able to handle being there alone with her without making love to her.

He hadn't realized what having her in his home was going to do to him. He couldn't remember the last time he'd had a decent night's sleep. As soon as he fell asleep he would dream about her, and those dreams were slowly driving him out of his mind.

During the day his thoughts would return to her; he would remember how she looked, what she wore, an expression on her face. She always seemed so damned glad to see him when he got home hungry and tired. Without asking, she would get something for him to eat and drink and would sit quietly with him, as though she were just content to be with him.

He wasn't used to someone who didn't make demands on him, who seemed to accept him and his lifestyle. He was finding it more and more difficult not to take advantage of the situation. Perhaps getting away today would help ease the tension for him.

"I haven't been to the park in a couple of years. I think that would be fun," she said, her eyes sparkling.

Michael fought the impulse to lean over and kiss her. She was such a temptation, and one he knew he wouldn't be able to resist much longer.

"I thought we might park near the island and go over by the rapids." He paused, studying her. "If you feel up to it, that is."

She laughed. "I feel like a fraud, actually. I'm really all right now. There's no reason for my not returning to work."

"Not right away, please. We're running down some fingerprints we found at the shop. We should be getting a report back in a day or two."

Sabrina felt that Michael was making too much of what had happened, and she discovered that she didn't want him worrying about her. Today she wouldn't think about anything but the fact that they were going to spend a few hours together.

Later she decided that the day would stand out in her memory as one of the loveliest she had ever spent. They explored several of the paths near the bluffs overlooking the island, enjoying the view and each other. Michael seemed to be more relaxed than she had ever seen him as they wandered around the Indian council area.

By the time they reached the rapids on the island, they were both ready to sit and rest for a while.

"I don't believe I've ever seen water this blue." Michael commented after a while. The source of the water was an underground river a few hundred yards from where they sat.

"I have a friend who grew up near here," she replied in a lazy tone. "She said that as a child she was convinced that there were little magic people who lived here at the park. She called them Tonkans. She decided that they came out at night, after everyone had gone home, and added bluing to the water to keep it looking like that.''

Michael was stretched out beside her, leaning on his elbows. ''Do you believe in the Tonkans?'' he asked with a grin.

She shrugged. ''It's as good an explanation as any. The color certainly doesn't look real, you have to admit. I think that whenever I come here I'm more aware of the Indians who lived in and around the area. Sometimes I feel as though—if I were quick enough— I would see one or more of them looking down at us from the bluffs up there.'' She pointed up to the towering bluffs, finding their sheer grandeur fascinating.

''Do you come here often?'' she asked after a while.

''Whenever I can.''

''I used to bring Jessica here all the time, but then her schedule became hectic and we got out of the habit of coming.''

He sat up so that their shoulders were touching. ''You really miss her, don't you?''

''Yes, I do, but I'm pleased that she's as independent as she is. I wanted her to be strong and self-reliant, willing to take chances, willing to grow and learn about life.''

''And what about you? Are you willing to take chances?''

Sabrina caught her breath at the sudden intensity in his voice. ''I suppose that depends on what I would be taking a chance on.''

He reached out and cupped his hand around the back of her neck. Just before his lips touched hers, he murmured, "Us."

Although tender, the kiss held a hint of passion that teased her with its power over her senses. He nibbled at her bottom lip, then stroked his tongue soothingly across it. When she responded to him, his touch became more intimate and exploratory.

Sabrina hadn't realized how much she had wanted him to kiss her again until now. She felt as though she had just gone up in flames.

He slipped his hand beneath her sweater and brushed against the lace of her bra. Finding the front clasp, he slowly turned it until the bra fell open. He gently cupped one of her breasts, sliding his fingers slowly back and forth until she could feel a tightening within her body in response.

His touch made her tremble and press closer to him. He lifted the sweater and placed his mouth over the rigid peak, his tongue lightly flickering across the sensitive crest of her breast.

Sabrina forgot that they were in a public park, no longer aware that anyone looking down from the bluffs would be able to see them. She was too caught up in the wonder of what she was experiencing through his touch.

He lazily moved his mouth to the other peak, his hand still gently holding the first. She could feel his hot breath on her sensitive skin and could not hold back a soft moan.

Michael paused, forcing himself to hold on to his restraint. What the hell was he doing? The purpose of the outing had been to release some of the tension that had been growing between them. This certainly wasn't the way to do it!

Reluctantly he refastened her bra and straightened her sweater. "I'm sorry, honey. I don't seem to be able to think straight when I'm around you."

He watched as her eyelids slowly opened, their slumberous sensuality almost destroying his tenuous hold on his willpower.

"Are you ready to go?" he asked, brushing a wisp of hair behind her ear.

She smiled and nodded. He stood and pulled her to her feet, then hugged her to him. They returned to the car in silence.

By the time they returned home, some of the tension had eased between them. More tired than she wished to admit, Sabrina accepted Michael's suggestion that she rest while he got some needed chores done outside.

He spent the afternoon raking leaves and chopping wood, hoping to burn up some excess energy before evening. He wasn't sure how he was going to get through the weekend without dragging her off to bed with him. He supposed the best thing to do would be to tell her how he felt, what he wanted, to be honest with her.

They were adults, weren't they? He was encouraged by her response. Maybe she was as attracted to him as he was to her.

Hours later, he still hadn't found a way to broach the subject of possible intimacy between them. They'd had dinner and, because the weather had turned cooler, he'd built a fire in the fireplace. Now they were watching a movie on cable television. He was stretched out on the sofa, and she was curled up in one of his overstuffed chairs.

The movie was all right, Michael decided, if you liked that sort of thing. *Terms of Endearment* was more of a woman's movie, he decided. The mother-daughter conflict didn't particularly interest him, but the acting was good, and he always enjoyed Jack Nicholson.

It was rather sad, too, so when it was finished he wasn't surprised to notice that Sabrina was crying. He had to admit it had brought a lump into his throat more than once.

He walked out into the kitchen to get something to drink and called back. "Would you like something to drink?"

"No, thank you. I think I'll go on to bed," she replied in a muffled voice.

He shrugged. That was probably the safest decision she could make. He walked back into the living room, flipped off the television and started downstairs to shoot some pool. Halfway down the stairway he paused, listening.

He heard muffled sobbing. She was crying. The movie had been sad, but would it have affected her so strongly? Was she comparing the relationship of the mother and daughter to her with Jessica? Surely not. She had mentioned earlier that she wanted Jessica to be independent of her.

What could be wrong?

He turned around and went up the stairway, past the living room and up to the bedroom. She was in bed, the covers pulled high over her shoulders, her head buried in her pillow.

He sat down beside her and touched her shoulder. "What's the matter, honey? The movie get to you?"

She caught her breath and lay there for a moment without moving. Then she slowly turned until she was facing him. "I'm sorry. I don't know what's wrong with me. I guess the movie brought back some memories I wasn't prepared for."

"About you and Jessica?"

She shook her head. "About my marriage."

That surprised him. "Care to talk about it?" He smoothed the covers over her and stroked her cheek with the back of his hand.

She sat up, placed the pillow behind her back and leaned against the headboard. Drawing a ragged breath, she sighed and shook her head. "I don't know why that story hit me so hard. I suppose I just got so caught up in what the daughter was feeling. It was so much like what I went through."

He took her hand. "Tell me."

She was quiet for several minutes, as though she were trying to collect her thoughts. "We were both too young to get married. Our parents tried to talk us out of it, but Danny was going away to school and I didn't think I could survive without him. Money really wasn't a problem—our college funds were intact—and they finally caved in." She gave him a rather watery smile. "I think they were afraid I'd get pregnant if they didn't. As it turned out, I got pregnant on our honeymoon, so didn't enroll in classes that fall. Instead I stayed home and played housewife and bride."

He took her hand and held it between his.

"Danny had a football scholarship. He was a good athlete, but an indifferent scholar. I used to do as much of his homework as he did. After Jessica was born I took a couple of classes when I could, but Danny was seldom home, and I hated going off and leaving her with just anyone."

Michael shifted so that he was leaning against the headboard beside her. He slid his arm around her and held her close, wishing he could take away some of the pain he heard in her voice.

"The summer after she was born, Danny became interested in stock-car racing. When he wasn't in class or involved in sports, he was either working on his car or racing it."

Sabrina suddenly realized that she was resting against Michael's chest, her hand idly smoothing the material of his shirt. She felt so protected in his arms, as though nothing could ever hurt her as long as he was there.

"At first I used to go to all the races to watch him, but the noise scared Jessica, and the dust and confusion didn't help. I began staying home more and more."

She shook her head. "Looking back, I realize how ill prepared we were for the responsibility of marriage and children. I didn't know the first thing about being a wife and mother. But I tried. I really tried to do all the right things. Somehow they just weren't enough."

"What happened?"

"It was a freak accident...a trial run. No one really understood how it could have happened. Danny lost control on a curve, hit the rail and flipped over. They said he was killed instantly."

"It must have been a horrible time for you."

"He had another girl with him that night. Someone he'd met at school. I guess they had been seeing each other for some time. I think everyone on campus knew about it except me. She witnessed the crash and became hysterical. Eventually I heard about it."

He held her snugly against him. Now he understood why the movie had affected her so strongly. She turned and slipped her arms around him. "I've never told anyone else the truth about Danny—not my parents or his, and most especially not Jessica. I'll never really know, but according to the girl, Danny was planning to leave me. She said they had talked about it several times."

"Oh, Sabrina." He held her for a long time, content to have her in his arms, touched by her willingness to share something so traumatic with him. Her openness gave him hope about their relationship.

Michael felt that he understood her so much better now. Of course she would be shy of relationships. Like him, she had found only pain. So she had devoted herself to raising her daughter and filling her life with safe pursuits.

Sabrina felt drained now that she had shared with Michael such a painful memory. Maybe she had needed to look at that relationship once more to realize that she was no longer that terribly young, inexperienced girl overwhelmed by circumstances. Perhaps she had allowed those early experiences to color her view of herself where men were concerned. She'd assumed that she had been rejected, discarded, replaced. From her vantage point now, she could see many other ways of looking at what had happened.

Michael had come into her life, and he had taught her so much. She had learned not to be afraid of her feelings. Today at the park he had made her aware of how much she wanted him to make love to her. Unfortunately, she was too inexperienced to know how to let him know that.

She could feel his heart pounding beneath her ear, and she became aware of his ragged breathing. She lifted her head and looked at him. The message in his eyes was unmistakable.

With a boldness that surprised her, Sabrina slipped her arm around his neck, drawing him closer, and kissed him. Her kiss held all the pent-up longing of years, and by the time it ended she knew that Michael could be in no doubt of what she wanted to happen.

"Are you sure?" he whispered when their lips finally parted.

She couldn't look at him. Instead she reached for the buttons on his shirt and began to undo them. With a chuckle that was almost a groan, he began to help her remove his clothes. "Do you have any idea how badly I want you?" he asked softly, his voice uneven.

"No."

He slipped between the sheets and pulled her against his aroused body. "Then let me show you," he muttered, before his mouth found hers once again.

Six

Michael wasn't sure he was going to be able to hang on to his control. Afraid that he was rushing her, he forced himself to slow down. She wasn't helping his control any. He could feel her light touch as she ran her hands along his bare skin. He groaned when her fingers brushed against his arousal.

He shifted until his mouth found her breasts. He heard her slight gasp as he tugged gently against the fullness. Her skin felt satiny to his touch. When he slid his hand down across her abdomen, past the tight curls at the junction of her thighs, he found her moist and ready for him.

He forced himself to hang on to his control long

enough to reach into the drawer beside the bed. With only a slight pause, he moved above her and took possession of her, easing himself into her warmth, forcing himself to go slowly until he was fully sheathed deep inside her.

She was trembling so much that he was afraid he had hurt her. Opening his eyes he raised his head from her breasts and gazed into her face.

She glowed with a radiance that defied description. Her long lashes brushed against flushed cheeks, and her smile caused him to catch his breath.

"Are you okay?" he murmured.

"Much better than okay," she responded, sounding breathless.

"I don't want to hurt you."

"You're not."

He couldn't wait any longer. His body demanded satisfaction, and he began to move, wanting to please her but afraid that his control was gone. He gathered her closer as he increased the pace. She met each of his thrusts with one of her own, her soft sighs of pleasure encouraging him.

He felt her convulsive shudders in the same instant that he fell over the edge of control and went tumbling into a maelstrom of intense pleasure and relentless completion.

For a few seconds he felt almost disoriented. Never had he responded to anyone the way he had just now. He realized that he must be crushing her, and with immense effort he forced himself to raise his head.

She tightened her grip around him, her ankles locked around his legs.

"I'm too heavy for you," he managed to say between breaths.

"No. You're just right." She slid her hands across the satiny sheen on his back, measuring the width of his shoulders with her hands, tracing the slight indentation of his spine down to his tailbone, gripping his buttocks and squeezing.

She felt dazed. Nothing in her experience had prepared her for what she had just shared with Michael. She had only made love with a boy, never a man. Never a man like Michael.

Sabrina couldn't believe what she had been missing all these years, and yet she was thankful that she had waited to share such a beautiful experience with him.

None of her dreams could compare with the reality of making love with Michael.

"Well, Daniel, it looks as though our plans are working," Jonathan pointed out with pleasure.

"So it seems. However, I was sorry that Sabrina had to suffer an injury."

"Yes. There are some things we can't control, no matter how much we wish we could. However, we managed to have her discovered quickly. She would have been much worse off had she been left there until her assistant showed up for work the next morning."

"I don't think Michael is conscious of the fact that he wants to marry her."

"I agree. Sabrina hasn't gotten that far in her thinking yet, either. But, of course, that is what each truly hopes for—that commitment, the long-term caring, the give-and-take of life."

"When do you think they'll discover how deeply they feel for each other?"

"Soon now, I'm sure. Our plan worked quite successfully. Now we only need to allow them to come to the natural and very normal conclusion that calls for a permanent and public acknowledgment of what they are feeling." Jonathan and Daniel smiled at each other, pleased with their joint efforts to help those on the earthly plane to experience the wondrous and transforming joy of love for another person.

Hours later, Sabrina surfaced from a deep sleep. She felt deliciously warm and very content. She attempted to move in order to stretch and discovered that she was effectively clamped by a muscular arm and leg to a very masculine body. Cautiously opening her eyes, Sabrina stared at a strong, firm jaw a couple of inches away.

Michael. She had spent the night with Michael. To put it more bluntly, she had spent the night making love with Michael. Gray light had been replacing the darkness of the room by the time they had finally fallen asleep.

She inched away slightly so that she could raise her head and look down at him. He appeared so vulnerable in his sleep. Thick lashes concealed his compelling eyes. His face looked relaxed, with only a few lines around his eyes and the edge of his mouth. His lips looked very tempting, and she ran her tongue over her own lips as though she could still taste him.

Sabrina had had no idea that she had such a sensuous side to her. The past several hours had been a rare education in lovemaking, in enjoyment of another person, in sharing herself fully with another human being.

She felt renewed, somehow... revitalized.

Carefully lifting his arm from around her, she wriggled out from under his leg.

"Where you going," he mumbled.

She smiled. "The bathroom."

"Umh." He rolled over onto his stomach, burying his head under the pillow.

When she came out of the bathroom, she discovered that he hadn't moved. *My hero,* she thought to herself, grinning. The sheet and comforter were tangled around his waist, revealing his muscular back and shoulders. One arm lay flung across her side of the bed.

Now that she was up, she was wide awake—and cold. The gray light hadn't gotten much brighter, because a cold front had moved in sometime during the night. Dark, lowering clouds swept the sky with more than a hint of snow.

How quickly the weather changed in Missouri. She was grateful for the warm weather that had been an amiable companion while they were at the park yesterday.

Shivering, she searched for a heavier sweater and some woolen pants, then went downstairs and started the coffee. She was glad to have this time to herself. She needed to think. She was still stunned by the decisions she had made in the past twenty-four hours. To decide to embark on a flaming affair after all her years of being carefully aloof from men was so out of character for her.

What worried her even more was that even now she didn't have any desire to go back and change her decision. Spending these days with Michael was like stepping out of space and time. It had nothing to do with the real world and her responsibilities there. She was taking time for herself for once in her life. Finally, after eighteen years, she was no longer responsible for anyone but herself. And if she chose to be irresponsible, then only she would have to deal with the consequences.

The fact was that she loved the man. She certainly couldn't have explained it to someone else, since she didn't understand her feelings herself. However, she no longer felt alone, battling life's daily challenges. Michael was there—reliable, stable, dependable.

She stood at the window and watched as the strong wind whipped the bare trees and listened as it howled around the corners of the house, accompanied by the rhythmic spatter of rain hitting the glass that towered two stories above her.

A perfect day to stay in bed.

How many times had she made that remark over the years? Today it took on a meaning that caused her to smile and glance up at the loft. She returned to the kitchen, poured two cups of coffee and quietly carried them upstairs. Placing one on each bedside table, Sabrina slipped out of her clothes and got into bed, tugging the comforter around her bare shoulders.

"I missed you." His voice was muffled by a pillow.

She smiled. "I brought us some coffee."

Slowly he stretched and rolled, gathering her into his arms. "I know. I smelled it. It smells wonderful. You smell wonderful," he added, nuzzling her neck.

"It looks like it may snow."

"Darn," he said without emphasis or inflection, nipping softly at her shoulder.

"What's wrong?"

"I can't do any of the things I planned to do today." He tugged at the comforter until she released it enough for him to slide it down to her waist. Leaning over, he lazily flicked the tip of her breast with his tongue. "Guess I'll have to find something else to do."

"We could always shoot pool," she said, fighting to maintain her concentration on the conversation.

"Mm-hmm." He moved to the other breast, kissing her, nuzzling and stroking the sensitive area.

"Or—" She gasped when his hand slid between her legs.

He lifted his head and looked at her, his eyes dancing with a mischievous light. "Yes?" He found his goal and began to stroke her. Her body responded automatically, her hips lifting toward him with each movement.

"Enjoy the— Oh, Michael!"

She couldn't think any longer. She could only feel what he was doing to her. He was driving her crazy! He seemed to know just where to touch her to create the most dizzying sensations.

By the time he entered her she was almost beside herself, pleading for release. She held him tightly to her, staying with him as he set the pounding rhythm that would take them both where they wanted to be. When they reached that pinnacle of sensation, they both cried out.

They lay in a tangle of sheets, pillows and comforter, her head on his chest. They were both trying to catch their breath, and Sabrina could still feel his heart thudding against her ear.

"That's quite a wake-up call you've got there, lady," he said between breaths.

"Me?" She raised her head, pushing her tumbled hair away from her face. "All I did was to bring you some coffee!"

He turned his head slowly, as though it took all the energy he could possibly muster, and looked at the cup sitting there. "Mmm. Coffee. Someday I might have enough strength to pick up the cup."

She giggled, and he grinned at the sound.

"It's probably cold by now."

He leaned up on his elbow and picked up the cup, took a sip and nodded. "Just right." Pulling himself up against the headboard of the bed, he tucked her next to him with one arm. "Thank you, love."

"You're welcome. For what?"

"For being you. For coming into my life. For being here with me now. For taking a chance on us."

"Not to mention bringing you coffee in bed."

"Especially for that." He kissed the top of her head, then lazily combed his fingers through her hair.

"Michael?

"Hmmm?"

"May I ask you something?"

"Ask away."

"What's the real reason you wanted me to stay with you?"

There was a long silence before he answered. "Do you think this was what I had in mind when I suggested you stay here?"

She could tell from his tone of voice that he was hurt that she felt she needed to ask. She added sensitivity to the list of traits she was learning to attribute to him.

There was another silence before she decided to answer him honestly. "The thought obviously crossed my mind, or I wouldn't have asked." She leaned away from him so that she could see his face. He looked grim.

"I wanted you somewhere that I knew would be safe. This was the only place where I knew you would have some protection. I did not plot and plan to seduce you, if that's what you're asking.''

"Don't you think we moved into this relationship a little fast?''

"Obviously you do." Michael reminded himself that she was the one who had let him know the night before that she wanted more than shared kisses. Otherwise he would be feeling as guilty as hell about now. The fact was that he had wanted her from the first night he'd met her. If he admitted that, would she consider him a lech?

"I'll admit my head is whirling, and the concussion I received has nothing to do with it. How could something like this happen so fast?''

He touched the end of her nose with his finger. "You're asking the wrong person, lady. I've never reacted this strongly to another woman. If I believed in them, I'd swear you'd mixed up some love potion that bewitched me.''

She nodded her head. "That's exactly the way I feel. I consider myself very sane, sensible, practical, and I don't hop into bed with men." She waved her hand to encompass the bed. "Yet here I am.''

"Are you sorry?''

She closed her eyes, thinking about the past several hours. Sorry? How could she possibly be sorry about what they had shared. She had to be honest with him and with herself.

She shook her head.

"Neither am I.''

"I'm just afraid this is going to make my life very complicated."

He hugged her to him. "Not if we don't let it. Let's take it one day at a time, okay? So maybe we've rushed things a little. I won't push you for a physical relationship if you're not ready."

Easy enough for him to say, she decided, after the night they had just spent. But how could they ignore what had already happened between them? How could they go back to the platonic roles they had played all week?

She supposed it was possible. At least it would give her time to think some of this through.

"Maybe that would be better," she said quietly.

He almost groaned out loud. He'd been afraid she was going to say that! Why the hell had he been so quick to offer that option to her? *Because you don't want to lose her now that you've found her.*

Good point.

Lifting her chin, he kissed her. It was a long, leisurely, lazy kiss, just to show her that he could accept her suggestion without any ill will. At least that was his intent, but somewhere along the way he lost track of his original intention.

Sabrina eventually broke away from him. "Michael! What was that supposed to be?"

"A platonic kiss?" he suggested.

She moved away from him. "Hardly." She eyed him uncertainly. "If we're going to put this relationship back on a more casual basis, I don't think we can share those kinds of kisses."

He grinned. "Good point." He glanced around, taking in the dreary day. "Why don't we go have some breakfast, then play some pool?"

"Sounds fine with me. Just don't expect to get much competition from me. I haven't played for years."

She might not have played for years, Michael decided a few hours later, but she must have been one hell of a pool player when she had played. As the afternoon progressed, he watched her regain her eye for a shot, get her feel of the table and her cue and steadily begin to make each turn count.

"Where did you learn to shoot pool?"

"At home. We had a pool table, and my brother taught me." She glanced up. "But that was years ago."

"You couldn't prove it by me."

She sank three of her balls in a row and lined up her fourth shot.

Michael had to admit to himself that he wasn't much competition for her today. He was having trouble concentrating. He kept being distracted whenever she leaned over to check an angle or line up a shot. The jeans she wore fit so snugly that whenever she leaned over it was all he could do not to reach over and smooth his hand across her taut, saucy bottom.

He was acting like a lovesick teenager. Not since his college days could he remember feeling this way. He'd spent most of the night and morning making love to her and he still couldn't seem to get enough of her. She would walk around the table, intent on the game, the light shining on her hair, and his heart would suddenly bob up into his throat. Then he would forcibly remind himself about their agreement to cool things between them.

The bulky knit sweater she wore was the same color as her eyes, and he would find himself staring into her eyes as though hypnotized.

"Your turn, fella. You miss this one and you're through."

He glanced up, a little embarrassed to be caught daydreaming, then looked at the table. She had one ball left, besides the eight ball. He had four, and she had left the cue ball in a lousy position for him to do anything. Quite intentionally, he was sure.

He managed to sink two before missing a shot, but she was right. She ended the game.

She looked so damned proud of herself that he almost laughed. They had been playing for hours, watching as the rain turned first to sleet, then, just before dark, to snow. It would probably melt by morning, but in the meantime it was a good evening to spend indoors.

"Had enough?" he asked.

"Me? You're the one who's losing."

"Yeah, well . . . you know how it is. I need to have some sort of incentive. Something to really make it worth my while to try to win."

"You mean a bet?"

"A little wager on the side never hurt."

"I don't have any money with me." She thought about that. "I suppose I could write an IOU."

"You're so certain you're going to lose, are you?"

"No, of course not! I'm just not one to gamble. I don't even buy state lottery tickets."

He grinned. "Quite the conservative, aren't you? Ah, well. You probably wouldn't care for my next suggestion, either."

"What?" she asked suspiciously.

"Strip pool."

"Never heard of it."

"Well," he explained with an innocent smile, "It's like strip poker. If you lose, you have to take off something you're wearing."

He stood there grinning at her. She knew what that grin meant. He was just giving her a bad time by inventing some preposterous wager. There was no such thing as strip pool. But then again, how would she know? And what would he do if—

"Okay, it's a deal."

She watched with a great deal of satisfaction as her response caught him off guard.

"I was just kidding, honey. I don't want to embarrass you."

She smiled. "Don't worry, you won't. However, you may find yourself red faced before long." It didn't take much to figure out that she was wearing a great many more items of clothing than he was. Perhaps he should have thought of that before making his brash suggestion.

The mood in the room changed. A sense of purpose and dedication began to settle in. They carefully followed the rules for picking the first player to break, and when Michael won Sabrina stood by and watched him run the table, winning the game without giving her an opportunity to shoot.

"Willing to call this off now?" he asked as she gathered the balls on the table for racking.

"Of course not."

"What are you going to take off?"

"My ring."

"What?"

She glanced up at him and smiled. Then she removed the ring from her right hand and motioned for him to shoot. Perhaps he was getting the idea. Whatever the reason, he didn't play the second game as well, although he managed to squeak by.

This time she took off her watch.

Michael set his jaw and began the third game. This time everything went against him and Sabrina won with no problem. She stood there, waiting.

"I'm not wearing my watch," he pointed out needlessly.

"I know."

"And I don't wear a ring."

"I can see that."

"Well, damn it, what am I supposed to do?"

"Be inventive."

Finally he smiled devilishly and pulled off one of his sneakers.

She nodded agreeably and proceeded to win the next three games in a row.

If nothing else, they had discovered that they both were highly competitive. The kidding around had stopped. They were taking each game—each shot—extremely seriously.

Michael was now playing barefoot, having lost the other shoe and both socks, while she was still fully clothed. He was determined to show her that he wasn't easily rattled.

They paused long enough to eat a couple of sandwiches, and she agreed to have a beer with him—an unaccustomed drink for her—but the tournament was the focal point of the evening.

Several more games were played and most of them went against Sabrina. She, too, was now without socks and shoes, and she had to decide what item to take off next. After a silent debate, she reached to her waist and unbuttoned her jeans, then slowly unzipped them. She took her time sliding them down her legs, then carefully stepped out of them. Nonchalantly she smoothed the hem of her sweater and said, "I believe it's your shot, isn't it?"

Michael could only stare. The silk-and-lace panties she wore hid nothing. Cut high on her thighs, they were too thin to conceal. They teased. Her legs were long and shapely, and as she stood waiting for him to finish she leaned against her cue, as relaxed as if she were fully clothed.

Damn her! How could he possibly concentrate with her standing around looking like that? He closed his eyes, forced himself to think about the game, then opened them and leaned over to line up his shot. As he looked down his cue, his gaze was directed to the V of her pastel panties at the other end of the table. He could feel his body reacting. What red-blooded male wouldn't react to that sort of provocation?

Michael lost that game. And the next one.

He was now down to his briefs, a bright red pair that concealed very little. If Sabrina won once more, he would be nude. And the loser.

Sabrina was feeling distinctly uncomfortable. She had had fun watching him squirm, seeing his forehead bead with perspiration during the last two games. She had even enjoyed viewing his bare chest as she had played the last one.

She was certain it was only the bright color of his briefs that she found distracting. The problem was that no matter where she lined up to shoot he seemed to be at the other end of the table in her direct line of vision. If she changed her mind and moved to another ball, he would also move. She couldn't get away from him.

Neither one of them had said more than a half-dozen words for hours.

How could he be so nonchalant—now that he was practically naked—about his obvious arousal? There was no way she could ignore it. That tiny red excuse for underwear hadn't been intended to cover such a situation.

For the first time in almost an hour, Michael was beginning to enjoy himself once again. It had been hell watching her bend over, leaving her derriere bare except for a tiny piece of lace. Or watching her stride around the table, her long legs reminding him of how they had wrapped around him so passionately the night before. Or having to stare at the V nestled at the top of her thighs.

Now it was his turn to watch her squirm. And squirm she did. He made sure he was always in her view, letting her see the effect she had on him. And when it was his turn to shoot, he did so with deadly accuracy, winning the game.

She removed her sweater, leaving her clad in only her lacy bra and panties.

Sabrina lost the next game and reluctantly unsnapped her bra.

He didn't really think he was going to be able to get through that last game. He watched her frown as she tried to guide her cue past her breast, which was no longer hidden from his sight. It was almost as though he could feel that satiny surface as the cue slid past— back and forth—as she positioned herself for the shot. His fingertips quivered with the imagined sensation.

"Darn it!" She had missed the shot.

"What's wrong?"

"I can't play without a bra. These get in the way." With a look of disgust, she lifted her breasts with her hands, as though trying to decide what to do with them.

He could think of several things he wanted to do with them. Immediately.

"Do you want to concede?" he asked, his voice carefully casual.

"No! I can still beat you!"

He smiled. "Go ahead and try, lady. I'm not stopping you."

He grew hotter with every movement she made. He could tell that she was determined to beat him now that the moment of truth was at hand.

She had played brilliantly all evening, making some shots that he had seen professionals miss, and she had been under considerable pressure. He had seen to that.

What a woman. Somehow he had to convince her that what they had together was too powerful to ignore. Whatever Fates had brought them together, they had found each other, and what they had found could never be duplicated. Not for him, anyway. Surely she felt the same way.

She sank the eight ball and spun around, triumphant. "I won, I won! I—"

As soon as he saw that the ball was going into the pocket, Michael made his move. His briefs were gone and he was striding over to her by the time she turned around.

"Michael!" Laughing, she allowed him to pick her up and seat her on the side of the table. But when he started tugging at her one remaining piece of clothing, she protested. "Hey, that's not fair! I won! I don't . . . have . . . to . . ."

Her words were lost as he pulled her legs around his waist and plunged deep inside her without saying a word. His mouth found hers, his tongue imitating his movements. She had teased him all evening, taunting him with her luscious beauty. He had been forced to look without touching, to merely imagine, to remember, to fantasize.

Winner or loser, agreement or no agreement—he had to have her. Now!

Seven

During the past two hours Sabrina had become increasingly aroused as Michael had revealed more and more of his well-honed body to her gaze. She had begun to have second thoughts about their agreement, wondering if they were being realistic with regard to their new relationship. His shattering response to the end of the game put an end to her confusion and delighted her with his intensity and spontaneity. The sheer unexpectedness of his move took her breath away, and his driving possession left her helpless to do anything but hang on to him.

He felt good to her. She let her hands roam up and down his back, feeling the muscles tensing and working in his buttocks, experiencing him with a sensitivity that had only recently developed. She could almost feel his pleasure in making love to her; she almost knew how desperately he had wanted her.

Suddenly he raised his head and let out a cry as he made a final driving lunge deep inside her. She responded with a strong, convulsive movement that seemed to go on and on within, holding him, stroking him, loving him.

"Oh, Sabrina!" he moaned, his legs shaking so badly he was afraid they weren't going to hold him much longer. He eased her off the table and lowered them both to the floor, where they lay in a limp tangle of arms and legs, their bodies still joined.

Neither one knew how long they lay there like that, just as neither one knew who chuckled first. Or was it a giggle?

Once it started, they both laughed long and hard.

Eventually Sabrina carefully moved off him and stretched out by his side as he lay spread-eagled.

"So much for our platonic relationship," he finally managed to mutter.

"Maybe we'll be all right if we don't play any more strip pool."

He lifted a brow. "Think so?"

She couldn't find an answer to that at the moment.

"I wonder what we're trying to prove?" he muttered after several minutes of silence. "How many times a couple can make love in twenty-four hours without killing themselves?"

"Do you think we've set a record?"

"No. I think we just killed ourselves."

Sabrina sat up, looking indignant—or as indignant as she could, under the circumstances. "Speak for yourself. I realize that a man your age has to take it a little easy—"

Michael's head came up with a snap. "A man my age? What a snide thing to say! I'll have you know that I—"

She leaned over and kissed his protests into silence. When she raised her head, they were both smiling.

"I have an idea," he offered.

She groaned. "I'm not sure I can handle any more of your ideas."

"You'll like this one. Why don't we fill the Jacuzzi in the upstairs bathroom? That should help to revive us."

"Either that or relax us until we melt."

He came to his feet, ignoring his lack of clothing, and pulled her to her feet. "Come on. You'll enjoy it. I promise."

Standing beside him, she casually ran her tongue over his nipple. He jerked as though he had just received an electrical shock. "See? There's still life somewhere in there," she pointed out, pleased with herself.

He took her hand and led her to the stairs. "You knew what you were doing to me when we were playing pool, didn't you?" he demanded.

She shook her head. "No. Not at first. It was only after you, uh, revealed yourself that I realized something must be getting to you. Since I'd only taken off my jeans, I wasn't sure what it was, but—"

"But you played the scene out anyway, right?"

She giggled. "I suppose."

He paused on the stairs and hugged her, then continued upstairs. After filling the tub, they sank into the bubbling torrent of water with sighs of pleasure. When he tugged at her hand, she willingly allowed him to guide her over to his lap. "I'm not trying to start anything, believe me. I just want to hold you close to me."

She snuggled against him, content, enjoying the moment. The real world had never seemed so distant.

The steady ringing of the phone intruded into their sleep. Michael fumbled for the receiver.

Sabrina fought her way through layers of foglike sleep and forced her eyes open. There was no light coming from outside. She glanced at the digital clock beside the bed and noted that it was almost five o'clock.

She listened to Michael's side of the conversation but couldn't tell much from it. He asked a few terse questions, gave some instructions, then hung up and threw back the covers.

"Trouble?"

He started toward the bathroom. "That's a given in my line of work."

She heard the shower running. He was obviously going to work early. She slid out of bed, dressed hurriedly and went downstairs. At least he could have some coffee before he left.

A hot cup of coffee waited on the counter when Michael walked into the kitchen. No matter how many times she saw him in his uniform, Sabrina still reacted to him. She turned away, embarrassed that he might see how strongly he affected her.

"You didn't need to get up," he said softly, coming up behind her and slipping his arms around her waist. He hugged her to him.

She leaned her head back against his shoulder and closed her eyes. He felt so good to her. "I wanted to make you some coffee."

He kissed her neck. "You're spoiling me."

She turned her head so that her lips brushed lightly against his. "You're easy to spoil," she whispered against his mouth.

He turned her in his arms and kissed her—a long, leisurely kiss that made her knees wobble.

When they finally paused for air, he grinned and said, "How about a friendly game of pool when I get home tonight?"

"How friendly?"

He chuckled. His smile was dazzling. "Very friendly."

She stepped back from him. "Mike, I really need to go back to work. I've been gone a week. What if someone needs me? I can't continue to hide forever."

"All right. Let me see what I can find out on the fingerprint inquiry we made. Maybe something's turned up."

"At least let me get in touch with Pam."

He kissed her again, then abruptly turned away and walked over to the counter, where his coffee waited. He drained the cup in three swallows, then refilled it before he faced her again.

"I have no problem with that, but I don't want you leaving the house. As soon as I find out anything, I'll call you."

"Whoever it was probably left the area the same day he broke into the shop."

"Maybe," Michael replied. "I just don't want to take any chances." He picked up his hat and started for the door. "I'll see you tonight sometime."

She smiled. "I'll be here."

The house seemed empty after he left, and Sabrina glanced at the clock. It was too early to stay up. She turned off the light and went back upstairs to dream about Michael.

It was after ten o'clock that morning before Sabrina called Pam at the shop.

"The Crystal Unicorn, Pam speaking."

"Hi. This is me."

"Sabrina! Am I ever glad to hear from you! I tried all weekend to get in touch with Mike to find out where you were, but he had the weekend off and has an unlisted number."

"Why were you looking for me?"

"Well, it started out because Jessica called. I knew you didn't want her to know about what happened, so I made up some excuse about your being away at the moment. She said she'd tried the house the night before until quite late, and when you never answered she became worried. She knew you seldom, if ever, stayed out late."

"Oh, dear." She had talked to Jessica the day she'd left the hospital. They had agreed not to get into the habit of calling each other frequently. What could have happened? "Did she say what she wanted?"

"I got the impression she wanted to tell you about a fellow she'd met. Nothing major...until she couldn't find you, that is."

"Oh. When did she call?"

"Friday."

"I'll call right away."

"Also, there have been several calls from your supplier in Arkansas. Rachel mentioned something about an order being put in your shipment by mistake."

"Did she say what it was?"

"It was a special order that someone in her shop had made up, and she inadvertently packed it with your things. She seemed really upset. I guess the guy who was supposed to have gotten it is raising all kinds of hell."

"What did the order look like?"

"Like most of her merchandise, it was blown glass. There were two leaping dolphins coming out of an ocean wave. I swear to you, I've taken this place apart, piece by piece, and I haven't seen anything remotely resembling that."

"Oh, Pam! I know what she's talking about. I came across it the morning after I brought all that stuff back. It's absolutely beautiful. The crystals in the wave catch the light so that the water actually seems to be moving. I took it home, thinking I would give it to Jessica for Christmas." She was quiet for a moment. "I remember thinking at the time how peculiar it was that there was no listing for that piece on the statement. I was going to ask Rachel for more of them the next time I go down."

"Well, maybe you should call Jessica and Rachel and calm them both down. It sounds as if it would only take a phone call to each of them."

"No problem."

"Now are you going to tell me where you've been?"

Sabrina smiled to herself. "Just taking your advice." Before Pam could ask any more questions, she said, "I'd better make those phone calls and find out what's going on. I'll call you later."

"But, Sabrina... Where are you? Are you at home?"

"I'll call you," she repeated, hanging up. She sat there for a moment, looking out at the lake. Her life was suddenly readjusting itself once again, and she realized more fully how out of character her behavior this past week had been. It was just not like her to completely lose touch with her work and her family.

Was it the blow to her head or being around Michael that had caused such a lapse?

She shook her head. Nothing in her life had been the same since the night Michael had approached her van upon her arrival from Arkansas.

Arkansas. That reminded her. She had to call Rachel. She found her address book in her purse and quickly flipped it open to Rachel's number.

As soon as Rachel heard her voice, she exclaimed, "Oh, Sabrina, do you have any idea how glad I am to hear from you?"

"From the sound of it, I could ask for a special discount on merchandise for the next twenty years and get it."

Rachel laughed. "You got that right. I tell you, I've really been in a dither. I have a new artist working with me these days. Wouldn't you know I would do something stupid with one of his creations and get him and his client furious? Please tell me you know where the dolphin figurine is."

"I do, I do, never fear. It's sitting on my dresser at the house. I was so impressed with the craftsmanship that I intended to give it to Jessica."

"Oh, thank God you have it. Look, the client is up in Osage Beach right now, trying to find you or someone who knows something. Would you mind if I call him and have him pick it up from you?"

"No problem. Since it's at the house, you might as well have him meet me there." She gave directions to her home, then added, "Do you think you can have your new guy make up some more like it? I could sell those little jewels like crazy up here.''

"I'll talk to him about it. I'm afraid I'm not his favorite person these days. Finding his treasure will no doubt redeem me, at least a little, in his eyes.''

"I hope so. I'm really sorry about all of this, Rachel.''

"Hey! It wasn't your fault. I'm the one who messed up. I'm just sorry to create such a hassle for you. Look, I'll call him right now and have him meet you in an hour or so. Will that give you enough time?''

"Sure. I'll be seeing you in a few weeks, Rachel.''

"Oh, Sabrina?''

"Yes?''

"Modeled your new sleepwear lately?''

"More than you can possibly imagine, my dear. I can't tell you how much I appreciate your gesture!''

"Sabrina! What's going on with you? You were shocked to the gills when you first opened that package.''

"Maybe I'll tell you the next time I'm down. Goodbye, Rachel,'' she added, laughing at Rachel's protests as she hung up the phone.

It was only after she hung up that Sabrina remembered her promise to Michael. She looked up the local number for the highway patrol in the phone directory and dialed hurriedly.

As soon as the phone was answered she asked, "May I speak with Sergeant Donovan, please?''

"I'm sorry, ma'am, he isn't in at the moment. May I give him a message?"

Darn. What was she supposed to do now? No doubt Rachel was already in touch with her irate client. Making up her mind, she said, "Yes, thank you. Would you please tell him that Sabrina Sheldon called? Tell him that I have to go to my house for a few minutes and that I'll be in touch with him later."

"Sure thing."

"Thank you."

Then it hit her that she had no transportation! Obviously her brain wasn't functioning full-time yet. Shaking her head, she called the shop again.

"Hi, Pam," she said as soon as Pam answered. "I really need a favor from you."

"That was quick. Did you get in touch with Rachel?"

"I did. The client who ordered the figurine is in town and wants it immediately. Unfortunately, I'm not at home and I don't have my car."

"No problem. I can come get you. Where are you?"

Here it comes. She gave directions, then said, "I'm at Michael Donovan's house."

The silence after her comment seemed to echo with questions.

"Mike's house," Pam repeated, her voice an octave higher than normal.

Sabrina chuckled. "That's right."

"Sabrina, I only suggested that you date the man, not move in with him. I mean, I could tell there was something going on between you two that day at the hospital...but let's face it, you hardly know the man."

"That's true."

"Well, far be it from me to give you advice about how to live your life...."

"Why? It never stopped you before."

"Oh, you!" Pam began to laugh. "I'll be there soon, okay?"

"Thanks, Pam. I really appreciate it."

"Don't worry. I intend to hear all the details."

Sabrina hung up and started upstairs. She needed to change clothes. At least now she could get something different to wear.

She wondered if Michael had gotten her message. Hopefully he wouldn't be too annoyed with her. She was sure that once she explained what had happened he would understand.

Fifteen minutes later, she heard a horn honk, grabbed her purse and ran downstairs. Waving at Pam, she locked the door behind her, then realized that she had just locked herself out of his house. Oh, well. There was nothing she could do about it now. She would call Michael later from her place and explain what she had done.

She climbed the wooden stairs from the front door to the driveway, where Pam waited in her car. As soon as Sabrina got in, Pam exclaimed, "My God, Sabrina, you look marvelous! If I'd known getting involved with Mike Donovan would do this for you I would have recommended it ages ago."

Sabrina felt her cheeks growing warm. "Don't be silly. Jeans and a sweater do not make a person look marvelous."

"No, but that glow about you certainly does. You just radiate vitality. My imagination is running overtime. Tell me all."

"There's not much to tell, actually. Mike wanted to be sure that I was somewhere safe while they were investigating the attempted burglary and assault on me, so he had me stay at his place. I haven't seen much of him all week. He works long hours."

"But I happen to know he had the past two days off. Surely you saw more of him then."

Sabrina could feel herself blushing, a sudden picture of their pool game flashing into her mind. "You could say that."

Pam glanced at her, then grinned, her eyes returning to the road. They had gone a few miles when Pam began to laugh.

"What's so funny?"

"I was just thinking about what Jessica's going to say when she finds out about you and Michael."

"Would you stop making it sound as though Michael and I are having some torrid love affair?"

"Are you going to sit there with a straight face and try to tell me that you have lived with that man for a week and he hasn't made love to you?"

Sabrina decided to sidestep the question. "What do you mean about Jessica saying anything, even if I am seeing Michael?"

"You have to admit that she's not used to sharing you with anyone and she's very possessive of you. She's grown up having your undivided attention."

"Was that so wrong?"

"Who knows? I'm just saying that she might not take too kindly to having to share you with anyone."

"She'll just have to learn how, then," Sabrina murmured.

Pam chuckled. "Good for you, boss lady. It's time you had a life of your own."

They pulled up in front of the house. The last time she'd been there she had been with Michael, and once again she felt a twinge of conscience. She shook it off. Now she would have her car. He'd have to let her know when he was home before she could get back into his house.

She also intended to dress very carefully to make sure that she wore a number of items of clothing that could be discarded without revealing herself, just in case he was serious about another game of pool.

After waving goodbye to Pam, she fished into her purse for her keys and let herself into the house.

The first thing she needed to do was to call Jessica. Even if she was in class, maybe someone would hear the phone and take a message. Sabrina didn't want her daughter worrying needlessly about her.

Pam's comment came back to her as she waited for the call to go through. She had never thought of Jessica as possessive. Why would Pam see her that way?

The phone was picked up on the second ring.

"Hello, darling. This is your mother speaking."

"Mom! Oh, I've been so worried. I've had visions of you being kidnapped or bashed over the head and left for dead or something. Are you all right?"

Was it possible that her darling daughter had a touch of the psychic in her? "Really, Jessica. You're either watching too much television these days or you should put that creative imagination to work. Have you ever thought about being a writer?"

"Mother, you're changing the subject. Where have you been?"

So now it was "Mother," was it? Jessica only called her that when she was irritated with her. So much for being concerned about her safety.

"I'm fine, darling. Really. I understand you were looking for me. What's your big news?"

"Oh, it wasn't all that great. Jeff Malone asked me to go to the dance after the next home game. He's in one of my classes, and I never really thought he'd noticed me."

"I take it you've noticed him."

"You bet. He's a doll. Blond, blue eyes. Wears his hair shorter than most. Somebody said he's been in the service. They thought he was a marine."

Sabrina's heart sank. Her daughter dating an ex-marine. Oh, dear God. Now what? "That sounds really, uh, well...what can I say? You like him, he noticed you, asked you out. Things must be looking up for you."

"Mom? Are you okay? You sound kinda funny."

"I'm fine, honey. Really. Look, I've got to go. I'll talk with you again soon. I'll want to hear about your date with Jeff." Actually, what she would like to do was to *accompany* her on her date with Jeff. Of course, she knew better. Jessica had to make her own decisions, use her own judgment, make her own— heaven forbid—mistakes.

It was at times like this that she wished there were such things as guardian angels.

"Wait, Mother. Don't hang up! You never told me where you were the other night. I called until two o'clock in the morning!"

"Since when have I had to report in to you, young lady?"

"Don't try to sound like a parent now, Mom, it's too late. You're hedging, you're dodging the question, and, frankly, you sound guilty as hell."

"Jessica."

"Am I supposed to guess?"

"Jessica!"

"You don't want to tell me that you spent the night with some guy, do you, Mom?"

"Jessica!" Her voice sounded strangled.

"That's okay, Mom. I understand. You dedicated your life to raising me. Now I'm gone. It's time for you to have a life of your own. If you've found someone you want to spend time with, I think that's wonderful."

"You do?"

"Of course I do. You're a mature woman. You know how to behave. You understand the pitfalls of modern dating. You—"

"Wait a minute. Isn't this the speech I gave you just before you went to college?"

"And you have a great memory! Yep, I think I got it down fairly accurately."

"You're making fun of me."

"Not at all, Mom. Actually, I'm pleased for you. And I know that when you're ready to talk about him you'll tell me everything. So just remember whenever you're out with him that whatever the two of you decide to do together your daughter is probably contemplating a similar decision."

"Jessica!"

"Bye, Mom. Just remember. Don't do anything I wouldn't enjoy."

When Sabrina put the phone down she stared at it as though it were a snake about to strike. What had happened to her sweet-natured, obedient, loving daughter? After two months at school she had developed an outlook that could take a person's breath away. Especially if that person happened to be her mother.

Don't do anything I wouldn't enjoy, my Aunt Minerva! A sudden picture of her and Michael lying beside the pool table the night before flashed into her mind, and she flinched. Would she want her daughter doing something like that?

Of course not. She was too young, too vulnerable—and her mother was being a hypocrite.

Sabrina knew that what had happened between her and Michael was premature. Had the circumstances been different, they would probably have dated for months before becoming intimate.

She hoped.

Sabrina wasn't at all sure, not when she considered the way she reacted to him. She didn't know where their relationship was headed. But there was a sense of rightness about the two of them being together. Meeting Michael had forced her to face so many of her fears. She hadn't been conscious of the fact that she had hidden behind her role of mother to Jessica all those years.

Thank God Michael had come into her life when he had. He'd taught her so much. About life...and love...and sharing herself with another person. He was right. They would take it one day at a time. After all, they had all the time in the world.

Eight

She didn't like the man the minute she laid eyes on him—and that was before he opened his mouth. As soon as he started speaking, her opinion of him rapidly deteriorated.

The doorbell had rung only minutes after she'd hung up the phone. Sabrina had hurried to answer the summons. When she opened the door, he stood there in a rumpled suit and a food-stained tie, greasy hair and a few days' stubble of beard.

"You Sabrina Sheldon?" he demanded.

For the first time it occurred to Sabrina that she had neglected to ask Rachel the name of the man who was coming to pick up the figurine. What if this man had nothing to do with Rachel? Michael's warning flashed into her mind. This person certainly didn't look like anyone who would appreciate the delicate beauty of the leaping dolphins.

"That's correct," she said, praying that her voice wouldn't betray her nervousness.

"You've got something I want."

"And that is?" Who was this man?

"Don't get smart with me, lady. You've wasted enough of my time. Just give me the dolphins and cut out the chatter."

At least he was the right person. Regardless of who he was, she was not going to allow him to put one foot inside her house. She forced herself to smile as pleasantly as she could under the circumstances and said, "Just a moment and I'll get it for you."

She turned away and began to shut the door behind her when he shoved the door open. She stumbled back against the wall. "I'm not playing games with you, lady. You ain't shoving no door closed in my face. Now go get it."

The ease with which he had moved her and the door frightened her. She was no match for this man. She almost ran to her bedroom and picked up the figurine from her dresser.

She had only taken a couple of steps away from the dresser when he appeared in her bedroom doorway. "I told you I would get it! There was no reason for you to follow me in here."

As soon as he saw the little figurine, he jerked it out of her hand and studied it intently. Slowly he began to relax. He smiled, displaying the fact that he had more than one tooth missing. She tried not to shudder.

"Yep, that's it, little lady. I've had a hell of a time tracking this thing down."

"I'm glad that you're pleased. I'm sorry to rush you, but I have several things to do today...." She motioned toward the door and felt a rush of relief when he started out of the room.

He walked into the hallway, with her following a safe distance behind. "Yep. Everything's worked out all right after all. I hate mistakes, you see. Just hate 'em. People learn not to make 'em around me." He glanced over his shoulder as he reached the door. "You know what I mean?"

She must have made the right answer, because he continued through the doorway without stopping. As soon as he stepped outside, she closed and locked the door, her heart racing. What a horrible man. He made her flesh crawl.

"Oh, Michael. I should have listened to you. I should have waited for you to come over here with me."

She peeked out the window to make sure the man was really leaving. He was crawling into his car, thank God. She was shaking. Now that it was all over and she was safe, she was falling apart.

The sound of another car pulling up drew her back to the window. A highway patrol car pulled up and stopped in front of the other car. Michael. Oh, thank God, he was here. She stepped outside to welcome him.

She watched as he got out of the car. Never had she been more pleased to see anyone in her life. Let him be angry at her. She didn't blame him. She would promise never to be so thoughtless again.

He came around the front of his car, and she waved, but he didn't see her. He was looking toward the other car.

Sabrina heard a double explosion and with a sense of horror saw Michael fall against the front of his car and slide to the ground.

Michael! She screamed and began to run. She heard another loud report and saw the man in the car pointing a gun at her. She fell flat on the ground and heard tires squeal and a car engine driven at high speed. Carefully raising her head, she saw the car disappearing down the road.

"*Michael!*" She jumped to her feet, but her legs didn't seem to want to move. She stumbled up the path to the driveway. He lay where he had fallen without moving. "Oh, dear God! Michael!" She touched his face. He felt clammy, and blood was spreading rapidly across his chest. She had to get help!

She looked up and down the road. There were no close neighbors at home this time of year. She ran back down the steps, burst into the house and dialed the emergency number.

"Highway Patrolman Michael Donovan has just been shot in front of my house," she said, then quickly gave directions. "Please hurry. And call the police!"

Then she ran into her bedroom, pulled the blankets and comforter from her bed and dashed back outside. She had to keep him warm. She had to keep him alive. *Oh, Michael. Don't die. Please don't die.*

The ambulance was there within minutes, and she rode with them to the hospital. Everything that could be done for Michael was being done. A surgeon was already preparing for surgery by the time they got him to the hospital. Both city and state police officials were there, asking for details of what had happened.

Sabrina felt numb. This really couldn't be happening. She was going to wake up in a moment and find herself curled up next to Michael in that big bed of his and realize that all of this had been a nightmare.

"Ms. Sheldon, I know you're upset, but we need some answers. You've got to help us catch the man who did this. Nobody shoots a law-enforcement person and gets away with it. We'll hunt him down, but you've got to help."

Haltingly she described the man and told them everything she could. She gave them Rachel's number, hoping that Rachel wasn't somehow involved in what had happened. She had no idea who the man was or why he had shot Michael.

Finally one of them said, "I think we've got enough to get started." To Sabrina he said, "Why don't you go on home, Ms. Sheldon, and get some rest? I know this has been an ordeal for you, particularly since you haven't been out of the hospital all that long yourself.''

"I can't leave. I've got to stay here with Michael. I can't leave him."

One of them patted her shoulder. "We'll check back on his condition later."

The other one said, "I'm really sorry about all of this, Ms. Sheldon."

"So am I," she murmured. "So am I."

The time seemed to drag by as she waited. No one seemed to know anything. Had he ever regained consciousness? Was he still in surgery? Couldn't anyone tell her anything?

One of the nurses paused beside her. "Dr. Jordan will no doubt come and speak with you when he's finished in surgery. He knows you're waiting for some word."

Sabrina could scarcely see the woman for the tears that kept flooding her eyes. "Thank you."

However, when Dr. Jordan found her, his news wasn't good. "We've done what we could, Mrs. Donovan. I'm not going to pretend that he isn't in very grave danger. We removed the bullets, but they did considerable damage." His gaze held hers. "We'll do everything in our power to keep him alive for you."

"Can I see him?"

"Not for several hours. He's still in recovery, and will be for sometime. Then you will only be able to see him for a few minutes."

"I'll wait, if you don't mind."

"Suit yourself. I'll let you know if anything changes." He walked away, and only then did it register that he had called her Mrs. Donovan. He thought she was Michael's wife. His family.

His family! She had to let Steve know. She didn't know anything about Michael's parents. But maybe Steve would know.

All she knew about Steve was that he attended Stanford. She went to the bank of phones. It was a start. Sabrina didn't know how long it took before she finally had Steven Donovan on the other end of the line, but she was fairly certain that she had talked to everyone who worked at Stanford, taught there or attended as a student.

When she heard his voice, her knees almost gave way in relief.

"This is Steve Donovan."

"Uh, yes. Steve. My name is Sabrina Sheldon, and I live at the Lake of the Ozarks, in Missouri." He didn't need her life history, for heaven's sake. Get on with it. "I'm, uh, a friend of your father's, and— Oh, Steve. Your dad is in the hospital, and they don't know—" She stopped and tried to swallow. "They don't know if he'll—" Her voice broke.

"What? My dad's ill? What happened? How long has he been sick? Why didn't someone call before now? Why—?"

"No, Steve. He was in good health until somebody shot him today."

"Shot him! Oh, God, no!"

"Yes."

"Is he still alive?"

"Yes, but the doctor isn't too encouraging. I didn't know who to call. Are your father's parents—"

"Both dead. He doesn't have any family—" his voice cracked slightly "—except me."

"Steve, can you come?"

"Do you think he'd want me to?"

"Oh, yes, Steve. Your father loves you very much. He's so proud of you. He misses you, and—"

"I miss him, too," he said gruffly.

"It's a little tough to get here by air. If you fly into Kansas City you can catch a commuter bus."

"Yes. Yes, I'll be there as soon as I can. What did you say your name is?"

"Sabrina. Sabrina Sheldon." She gave him her home and work numbers. "I will probably be here at the hospital when you get here." Unless he arrived too late. But she wouldn't say that. She wouldn't even allow herself to think it.

"Thank you for calling me, Sabrina. You'll never know how much I appreciate it."

His deep voice sounded so much like his father's that she had to bite her lip—hard—to keep from sobbing.

"I'll see you, Steve."

"Mrs. Donovan?"

Sabrina opened her eyes and saw the nurse standing in front of her. Coming to her feet, she asked, "Is he—?"

"He still hasn't regained consciousness, but he is now out of recovery and in a private room. The doctor said you may see him, but only for a few minutes."

Forcing herself to stay calm now that she was going to be allowed to see him, Sabrina followed the nurse down the quiet hallway. She glanced at her watch. It was after midnight. She had been at the hospital since around three. Nine hours. It seemed like a lifetime. But not Michael's life. Please, God, don't take him now.

The nurse pushed open the door and motioned for her to go inside, leaving her alone with him. A night-light placed the room in shadows, and she slowly approached the bed. She saw why there was no one with him. He was hooked up to so many machines that there was no reason for anyone to hover over him. No doubt the nurses were watching the signals bleeping across the various screens at their station.

The covers were pulled up over his chest, and there were tubes going into his arm. So many wires and machines working to keep him alive until his body could take over the job.

Would his body do that? Please? Please get well. His hair looked stark against the white pillowcase, and she remembered how he had looked the other morning, with his head buried beneath his pillow.

There was no color in his face, except maybe gray.

"Oh, Michael. I'm so sorry for what happened. If I hadn't called and told you where I was, you wouldn't have come to the house. This is all my fault." She fought back a sob. "I don't want to lose you, now that you've come into my life."

She touched his cheek. "I love you, Michael. I want you to know that. There's so much I love about you ... your kindness, your gentleness, your understanding. Even your protectiveness. I've never felt so comforted as I have this past week. You're such a good, kind man ... filled with compassion. Please get well."

He was so still.

"I called Steve today. He's coming to see you. He loves you, too. It was so obvious in his voice. We have that much in common, anyway." She tried to swallow around the knot in her throat. "I want you to get well to give me hell for leaving the house."

The tears were sliding unheeded down her face. She didn't care. "I'm going home now for a couple of hours. I can't go back to your place, because I locked myself out. It's just as well. I couldn't stand to be there without you. But I'll be back. I want to be here for you. I want you to know how much I love you." Tears ran down her cheeks.

She heard the door open and turned her head. The nurse stood silhouetted in the doorway, and Sabrina slowly walked to the door, leaving Michael with the machines watching over him.

"Surely there is something that I can do, isn't there?" Jonathan asked his exalted leader.

"No, Jonathan. Your mission is to counsel Sabrina. What happens to Michael is not your concern!"

"But, sir. I don't think he's going to make it."

"I know."

"I don't understand."

"What has happened was something that was scheduled into his life program. What happens now will be up to him."

"But, sir, surely he won't let himself die at this point in his life! Not when he has so much to live for!"

"Die, Jonathan? Where did you get such an archaic expression? Nobody dies, Jonathan. You know that."

"Yes, sir. I was thinking in Earth language. But they've just found each other, after all this time."

"And I want to commend you on your inventive schemes. I thought the deer a nice touch."

"But shouldn't they have some time to spend together?"

"Time? Another Earth expression. They've been together before. They'll be together again. My, but

you've gotten quite caught up in the drama of the situation, haven't you? If Michael makes his transition now he will find many things to do while he waits for her to join him."

"It just seems so unfair, sir. I mean, Sabrina is just now beginning to truly understand herself and her relationship to her daughter, to find meaning in a relationship with Michael. This is such a cruel blow for her to have to endure."

"But you and I know that there is no such thing as 'losing' love. Love is a permanent condition, one that we carry with us at all times. She will always experience the love she feels for Michael. Sabrina will never be deprived of that."

Jonathan shook his head sadly. Gabriel certainly saw the overall picture better than anyone, but this time Jonathan hoped that something would happen to prolong the happiness that Sabrina and Michael had discovered on Earth.

Jonathan felt so helpless. All he could do was sit with Sabrina, wait and watch, and console her whenever he could.

"Excuse me . . . the nurse said you're Mrs. Donovan?" He sounded young, uncertain and bewildered.

As soon as she heard his voice, she looked up. Now she knew what Michael had looked like twenty years ago. She stood, holding out her hand. "You must be Steve. I'm afraid I've never bothered to introduce myself here. Since I arrived with your father, they just assumed . . ." Her voice trailed off.

The young man nodded. He was dressed fashionably in baggy pants and jacket. He wore his hair short in front and down to his collar in back. He was as tall as his dad, but not as filled out. Even though his eyes were blue, they were shaped like his father's, with the same unwavering look.

It was all she could do not to throw herself into his arms and just hold him.

"How is he?"

"His condition remains unchanged." She shrugged. "Whatever that means."

"Has he been conscious at all?"

"No. I must warn you that when you first see him with all those machines you may wonder if he's even alive."

Steve nodded, swallowing. When he ran his hand through his hair in a gesture she'd seen his dad use often she felt the tears well up in her eyes.

"Do they let you see him very often?"

"Once an hour. For just a few minutes."

"But he doesn't know you're there?"

"Maybe he does. I don't know. But I talk to him anyway. I tell him everything I want him to know. I want him, on whatever level he happens to be at that moment, to know that he is loved and wanted right here."

He took her hand. "I'm glad he's got you. I'm sorry to say he's never mentioned you."

"We haven't known each other very long."

He looked relieved. "Oh, well. That explains it. I haven't talked with him since August."

The nurse paused at the door of the waiting room. "Mr. Donovan? If you would like to see your father now?"

"Yes. Thank you." He squeezed Sabrina's hand before releasing it.

She sat down and waited for him to return. Now she didn't feel so alone. They could wait together.

Steve let himself into the room and stood by the door, staring at the man lying so still on the bed. Seeing him made the news become more real, somehow. He moved closer, looking at the man who had been a part of his world for the first ten years of his life.

What could he say to him? If his father were conscious and could hear him, what would he want him to know?

Steve looked down at his father's hand, which rested so quietly on his chest. He'd always remembered his dad's hands—their strength, their gentleness.

Only then did he realize that tears were running down his cheeks. He reached over to a box of tissues beside the bed and wiped his face.

He cleared his throat and began to speak in a low, hoarse voice.

"Hello, Dad." His voice sounded harsh in the quiet room. He cleared his throat again. "I guess you're kinda surprised that I showed up here after all these years." He reached down and touched his dad's hand and found its warmth reassuring.

"I had several hours to think on the plane flying out here, remembering things about you. It was surprising, all the things that came back to me. I remember when I was little, how you used to always let me sit on your shoulders, during parades and ball games and things. I remember thinking how lucky I was because I had the tallest father around."

He sank into the chair beside the bed and studied his father's face.

"You know, Dad, you always stood tall to me. I remember being so proud of you in your uniform. And sometimes when you'd come home you'd look so tired, and maybe, you know, sad, as though things didn't always work out the way you hoped they would on your job."

He paused, listening to the steady blips of the monitors, wondering if his father could hear him. He squeezed his hands together, praying that somehow his father knew what he was trying to say.

"Do you remember how you'd always let me crawl up in your lap, even after I was in school, no matter how tired you were, or how many hours you'd been working? You'd let me sit there with you. I always felt so safe there in your arms. I knew that nothing could ever hurt me because you were there."

Steve reached for more tissue and wiped his cheeks once more.

"And you came to all my ball games whenever you could get away. Did you ever know what a thrill it was for me to look over at the stands and see you sitting there watching me, smiling, giving me that thumbs-up signal?''

His voice cracked, and he paused, swallowing a sob before it became audible.

''I remember when Mom and I left and moved to California. I didn't think I could stand leaving you. I didn't want to go. But there was Mom. She was always so upset. And she needed me. She said that you didn't need anybody. But I wasn't sure about that. I'll never forget the sad look in your eyes, even though you didn't say anything to me about wanting me to stay, not wanting me to leave. You hugged me and told me you loved me.''

He fought for a calming breath.

''You know what I realized coming out here on that plane, Dad? That I'm twenty years old and I don't even know if my dad knows I love him. I couldn't remember the last time I told you. It was easy when I was little. We used to make a game of it. Then when I got older I was embarrassed about saying it, and you didn't seem to mind. You just seemed to know how I felt and it was okay.''

Steve could no longer sit still. He got up and paced across the room and looked out at the night. His throat felt raw. It ached from the effort at control. Finally he turned back to Michael.

''So I flew two thousand miles to tell you that I love you, Dad. I always have. I want you to know how sorry I am that I haven't spent more time with you during these past ten years.'' He placed his hand over

Michael's hand. "I have no one to blame but myself.
You offered to pay my way, but I was always so busy
with my own activities. You never put any pressure on
me. You always seemed to understand."

Steve shook his head in bewilderment.

"It was me who didn't understand. I guess I thought
I would have all the time in the world to see you, to be
with you, to get to know you better. I mean, as far as
I'm concerned you're invincible. Right up there with
Superman. It never occurred to me that you couldn't
stop bullets. That you were mortal. That you could die
and leave me. That I might never have the chance to
tell you how much I love you."

He could no longer hold back the sob that shook
him. He turned away, trying to gain control over his
emotions. He managed to take a couple of deep
breaths, then turned to Michael again.

"I have no idea if you can hear me or not, but
Sabrina said she talks to you anyway. I liked that. I
like her, Dad. She's real and she's loving. You need
someone like her in your life. We all do. I want to be
a part of your life, Dad. I want us to spend time together. I want you to be around when I get married. I
want you to help spoil your grandchildren."

Steve lifted Michael's hand and placed it between
his hands. He closed his eyes and whispered. "Oh,
Dad. I don't want you to die."

Nine

___

Doctor, this is Sue Brown, supervising nurse in ICU. Mr. Donovan is showing some increased activity on the monitors. It appears that he may be coming out of the coma." She listened for a moment. "Yes, sir. I'll tell them."

With a smile, she went to find the two people who had been living in the waiting room for the past few days. As usual, she found them talking quietly in the corner.

"There are indications that Mr. Donovan is regaining consciousness. The doctor will be here shortly to check him. He wanted you to know." She returned to her desk and left Sabrina and Steve staring at each

other, afraid to believe what they had just heard. Then
Steve gave a whoop and grabbed Sabrina, swinging
her around in a circle.

"Did you hear that? He's going to make it. I knew
it! He's too tough to let a couple of slugs in the chest
stop him."

Sabrina shuddered at the graphic reminder and the
memories it evoked. She had gotten to know Steve
quite well during these past few days, since they had
had little to do but wait and talk. One thing she had
quickly discovered—subtlety was not one of Steve's
long suits. He said whatever was on his mind, with
little regard for the consequences. How ironic that he
had chosen the field of communications in which to
work toward a degree.

He went charging after the nurse. "Can we see
him?"

She shook her head. "Not until the doctor ar-
rives."

"But wouldn't he want to see someone he recog-
nizes when he comes to?"

"You'll have plenty of time to be there when that
happens. He's far from being conscious. But he is
rousing, and that's an excellent sign."

Sabrina felt a wave of weakness wash over her, and
for a moment she thought she was going to faint.
Michael had somehow faced the crisis stage and had
hung on. Surely now he was going to be all right.

He had to be. Things would be different for him
now that Steve was here. Steve had spent all these

hours sharing his feelings about his father. He wanted a second chance to get to know Michael better.

She just wanted him to live and be a part of her life in whatever way he chose to be. She was no longer afraid to face her feelings about life and about him.

Three days passed before Michael was fully conscious. He sometimes stirred and muttered, but he didn't seem to be aware of his surroundings.

On the fourth day Sabrina and Steve were standing beside his bed watching him when he finally opened his eyes and looked around. He blinked several times, as though the light bothered him. Then his eyes narrowed and he looked at the man standing there.

"Steve?" His mouth formed the words, but no sound came out. He licked his lips and tried again. "Is that you?"

Sabrina thought Steve's smile was going to split his face. "Yes, Dad. It's me."

Michael looked bewildered. His gaze wandered to Sabrina. "Hi," he whispered.

"Hi yourself."

"How long have I been here?"

"I lost track of time. I honestly don't know."

"I vaguely remember somebody telling me I was shot."

"Yes. I understand that they caught the man who did it."

He lay there, a puzzled frown on his face. "I don't remember much about it."

She smiled. "Don't worry about it. The important thing is that you're getting better. You've amazed the doctors with your rapid progress."

He looked at Steve as though he were having trouble believing his son was there. "Shouldn't you be in school?" he finally asked.

Steve shrugged. "I can make it up."

"It's good to see you." He closed his eyes. He felt so damn weak. He could feel tears forming. The last thing he needed was to let his son see him cry.

"You're tired. We'll let you rest," Sabrina said, touching his hand lightly.

He opened his eyes once more. "You'll come back?" His gaze went to each of them.

Steve nodded. "You couldn't keep us away."

"I wouldn't want to try."

A week later the nurse had him sitting on the side of the bed. Dangling, she called it. Michael couldn't get used to feeling as weak as he did. He hated it. The pain in his chest still took his breath away. But at least he could breathe.

The doctor had told him that his chances had been slim. They weren't sure what had pulled him through. The doctor mentioned his strong constitution, his relative youth, his good overall physical condition.

He didn't mention love.

Michael wasn't sure where he had been. But he had been safe, hiding from the pain, waiting to see what would happen next. While he had waited there in the place of safety, his son had joined him. They had reminisced, reviewed their lives together and apart. Discussed their feelings about life in general, shared their philosophies. He had been comforted and warmed by his son's obvious love and tenderness, his compassion. They had discussed his choices. Did he really want to confront the pain? Wouldn't it be easier to ignore it?

Sabrina had kept visiting his safe place, as well. She had reminded him that he had taught her so much about love and that she wasn't through learning yet. She needed about thirty more years of tutoring, and he had to be the one to teach her.

When had all that happened? And where?

The nurse complimented him on managing to sit on the edge of the bed without falling off—as though he were a toddler in need of praise—plumped up his pillow, helped him to lie down again and promised him his lunch before she disappeared out the doorway.

When he heard the door open again, he thought he was going to be exposed to some more cheerful chatter. He almost didn't open his eyes, hoping she would leave him alone, but something different had entered the room, a new energy, almost as though the very air around him hummed.

Sabrina stood at the foot of the bed.

"Did I wake you?"

He smiled. "No. I was pretending, in case you were Chatty Cathy coming back for something." When she looked puzzled, he explained. "You know, the friendly nurse."

"She has a terrific crush on you."

He groaned and rolled his eyes.

"She does. She envies me."

"I do, too. You get to walk in and out of this place. I'm trapped here."

"Not for much longer. The doctor is extremely pleased with your progress. He's muttering something about miracles under his breath."

As soon as she got close enough, he took her hands, pulled them to his mouth and kissed each palm. He felt the slight tremor in her fingers and glanced up.

She smiled but didn't say anything.

There was so much he needed to say—so much that he needed her to know.

"Did Steve get off all right?"

"Yes. We made it to the airport with time to spare."

"I really appreciate your driving him into Kansas City."

"I wanted to do it." She brushed her hand across his forehead, gently brushing his hair back. "He's quite a guy. A son to be proud of."

"I know. It's still hard for me to realize that he actually came all this way to see me."

He hated the way his voice kept breaking, as though he were an adolescent whose voice hadn't quite found its true register.

"He loves you very much, you know."

Michael couldn't restrain the smile that appeared on his face. "Yeah. He told me."

"Do you remember my telling you that?"

His gaze met hers. "That you love me?"

She nodded.

He glanced down. After a moment he said, "I was afraid I dreamed it." His voice was so low that she barely heard him.

"I'm not sure I'll ever forgive myself for putting you in danger," she murmured, wanting to hold him in her arms and revel in the fact that he was alive and with her once more. "It just never occurred to me that the man Rachel told me about had anything to do with the break-in at the shop."

He pulled on her hand with a steady pressure until she was seated on the bed beside him. "You're changing the subject." He watched, fascinated as the color rose in her cheeks. "Do I still make you nervous, Ms. Sheldon?"

"A little."

"I find that hard to believe. A pool hustler like you nervous?"

Her soft laughter seemed to wrap him in a soothing warmth.

"Sabrina?"

Her eyes seemed to hold the light in the room. He was mesmerized.

"Yes?"

"I love you."

Because her hand was still between both of his, he felt more than saw her reaction.

"And you love me."

She nodded, as though she were unable to speak.

"And usually..." He paused because he felt her tense. But he couldn't let her reaction stop him from saying what he had to say. "Usually," he went on, "when two people love each other, they decide to get married."

He waited, but she still didn't speak. Her eyes seemed filled with emotion, and he could only hope that he would hear the answer he wanted.

"So what I've been wondering is, would you consider marrying me? That is, once I get out of here."

"Oh, Michael," she whispered.

He waited. And waited.

"Is that a yes?"

"I love you so much."

He grinned. "Must have been a yes."

"But it's so soon."

"To get married? Or to know that's what I want?"

She shook her head. "This has been such a traumatic time for you."

He frowned. "Do you think it's because I'm laid up here and don't have anything better to do that I decided to propose to you?"

"Not exactly, it's just that—"

"You know where I was when you called the day I was shot?" He didn't wait for her answer. "I'd taken my lunch break and was looking at engagement rings." He lifted her hand and looked at it. "I was trying to get some idea of what you might like, although, of course, I didn't know your ring size. But I did know I was going home that night and tell you that I didn't want any misunderstandings between us, that my intentions were strictly honorable, but that I was willing to wait as long as you needed in order to be sure about your feelings."

She leaned over and kissed him. "I'm very sure about my feelings."

"Then you'll marry me?"

"Yes."

"When?"

"Whenever you say."

He grinned. "That's what I like. A docile, accommodating woman."

"I'll let you get away with that because you're still in a delicate condition."

"Speaking of which—" He paused, as though searching for the right words.

"What do you mean?"

"Uh, delicate conditions. The one thing we didn't discuss was the possibility of pregnancy."

Sabrina's gaze didn't waver. "I know."

"It would be foolish of me to assume you were protected."

"Michael. I'm not pregnant."

"Oh."

She studied him for a few moments. "You look almost disappointed."

"Well, it wouldn't really be fair to you to have you start off our marriage being pregnant."

"You *are* disappointed!"

He'd had many long hours to think about Sabrina and their relationship, to remember the time they had spent together. It was only when he smilingly relived their unusual pool game that he realized he had not taken time to protect her as he had the night before. He'd been so caught up in what was happening at the moment that he hadn't given a thought to the possible consequences.

Lying in the hospital had given him plenty of time to think—and to consider what those consequences might be.

He'd fantasized about having another child, maybe more, with Sabrina. He would lie there when the pain seemed to gnaw at his chest like a starving rodent and visualize what it would mean to him to have another chance at being a husband and father.

Ten years was a long time to contemplate the mistakes he'd made. He knew what he would do differently if given the chance. But that was how he felt. He didn't know how Sabrina felt about the possibility of motherhood again. After all, she had raised her daughter. Perhaps now she wanted her freedom. Reluctantly he had allowed his dreams of a family to fade, at least until he knew for sure if she was pregnant and how she felt about the possibility.

"No," he finally replied. "Not really." Not exactly.

They looked at each other for several minutes without speaking. "I would very much like to have your child, Michael," she said quietly.

"You would?" He couldn't hide the hope in his voice.

"Yes."

He watched her expression as he asked, "So if you got pregnant right away—"

"I wouldn't complain."

He glanced around the room as though assessing their chances for privacy.

She began to laugh. "But I want you a little stronger than you are right now, my love."

He smiled, liking the idea that he was her love. "I was just bluffing," he admitted. "I'm so weak I can hardly feed myself."

She leaned down and kissed him very gently on the mouth. "We have plenty of time."

"I wonder what Steve and Jessica will say," he said after a moment.

"I won't try to guess. We'll let them surprise us."

"You really don't care, do you?"

"I care. But their opinions won't change what I do with my life and how I live it. I love you. I want to marry you, and if our marriage is blessed with a child I will be delighted. Whatever reaction that causes in the family they can deal with."

He groaned. "God! This is frustrating, lying here, wanting you so badly I ache with it and not being able to do a damn thing but look at you."

"Well, you could fill me in on what's been happening regarding that man who shot you. Did you get any more information about the shooting? I never understood why he shot you when he already had the figurine."

She was right. They needed to change the subject for the time being. But at least he knew where he stood with her now, knew he could spend his time lying there making plans for their future. He liked that thought very much.

He kissed the tips of her fingers and tried to concentrate on her questions. "He thought I was there to arrest him, according to Jim Payton, one of the men who worked on the case with me."

"Was he wanted for something?"

"He was part of a ring of jewelry thieves who had worked out an ingenious plan to smuggle diamonds out of the country. Unfortunately, through a quirk of fate, one of the shipments was sent to the wrong place."

Sabrina stared at him in disbelief. "Are you saying that the dolphin figurine contained diamonds?"

"That's right. They were scattered in the wave that had been shaped around them."

"That's what made the water glitter so! I thought those were crystals, since Arkansas has so many of them."

"That's what they were hoping anyone looking at the figurine would think."

"No wonder that was such a beautiful piece of work. It must have been worth a fortune."

"Several hundred thousand, anyway."

"So he was the one who broke into the shop, wasn't he?"

"Yes. He was a little careless. He left a print that helped us to identify him. When I got your message I had just found out the man's identity, but we had no idea where to look for him."

"How strange that you should have turned up at my house at the same time. Do you have any idea how upset I was when he shot you because of me?"

He pulled her closer. "You should have been. If you'd done what I asked, you would have still been at my home, safe. I was more then a little irritated with you by the time I got to your place."

"You had a right to be. I kept thinking about that all the while you were unconscious and we didn't know if you were going to pull through. I had no idea that there was any connection between Rachel's client and the break-in at the shop. Did Rachel know about the diamonds?"

"No. We discovered that he had blackmailed the artist to hide the diamonds in the figurine. The artist was more than cooperative once he knew about the arrest."

"I'm so glad that Rachel isn't in trouble."

"Me too. She has great taste in sleepwear."

She leaned over and kissed him. "I haven't even worn it yet."

"I know. I can hardly wait."

"Soon, love. Soon."

"I would like to have a word with you, Jonathan," Gabriel intoned.

"Yes, sir?"

"I understand that you contacted Michael Donovan while he was in a comatose state."

"Well, yes, sir. I did. I couldn't find anything in the statutes that forbade it, sir."

"Your behavior was highly irregular. What did you say to him?"

"Oh, I, uh, just introduced myself, and we chatted, sir. I explained my role in Sabrina's life, shared with him some of the more hilarious moments I've had trying to work with her independent streak. I told him how long I had worked to finally bring about a meeting between the two of them. You know, just chitchat.

"We also talked about Steve and all he meant to him. I, uh, even apologized for not being able to warn him about what happened."

"How did he take the information?"

"Quite well, actually. He was aware by that time that he was in a position to make a choice about whether to return to his earthly existence or whether to complete his transition."

"I suppose you did your own persuading."

Jonathan shone with a radiant light. *"No, sir. I didn't have to. Sabrina and his son did all the work,* sir. Their strong, steady love for Michael gave him the energy and strength to face the return to pain and a lengthy convalescence. My visit was more a getting-acquainted one. As you know, sir, he will never consciously remember anything we talked about. It is all deeply buried in his subconscious.''

Gabriel was silent. ''I know that, but his not remembering it is not the point, as you well know,'' he said finally. ''He had Daniel working with him, and you should never have interfered.''

Jonathan waited, not knowing what he could say to redeem himself in his superior's eyes.

''Well,'' Gabriel went on after a lengthy silence, ''I must say your behavior has been more than a little unorthodox, but given the situation I suppose it was understandable.''

''Yes, sir.''

''I suppose I should be pleased with the enthusiasm you have shown for your job. All in all, you managed to pull the whole thing off quite nicely.''

Jonathan beamed. ''Thank you, sir. Daniel was also a great help.''

''So he was. But Daniel wasn't the one breaking all the established traditions for conduct. I sincerely hope that this doesn't happen again.''

''Oh, yes, sir! I mean, no, sir. What I mean to say—''

''I'm aware of what you're trying to say, and I heartily concur. We both know that Michael is going to have his hands full trying to deal with Sabrina's *spirited ways. He doesn't need to deal with your well-meaning interference again."*

"Yes, sir."

"Yes, well, get back to work, then."

"Yes, sir."

"Oh, and Jonathan?"

"Yes, sir?"

"Congratulations. You have certainly earned your promotion."

Jonathan watched as the brilliant light dimmed around him and knew that Gabriel was no longer there.

Promotion or not, he would be with Sabrina for some time to come. He was rather looking forward to it, actually.

He rubbed his hands together. Twins. Just what they needed for a new little family. This was going to be fun.

Epilogue

When he walked into the bedroom he found her standing before the sliding glass door that led out to the lanai. The only light came from the full moon that coated the nearby gently rolling waves and the white beach with silver dust.

She wore the gown that he had first seen the night he had met her, and she looked as good in it tonight as she had when she'd first worn it for him—on their wedding night, five years ago tonight. It cupped her full breasts and skimmed her trim body but did nothing to conceal what lay beneath it.

Her hair tumbled around her shoulders, framing her face. It was longer now than when they had first met.

Its glorious color lit up any room she happened to enter.

As usual, when Michael saw her he seemed to need more air and his heart began thudding in his chest. After all this time he still had trouble believing that she was his. He felt as though he had waited for years— no, a lifetime—for this beautiful woman.

Silently approaching her, he slipped his arms around her waist and pulled her against his bare body.

"It's all so beautiful, Michael," she whispered, as though afraid to disturb the scene before them.

His lips found the soft, vulnerable spot just below her ear and caressed her, causing her to shiver.

"I've always wanted to visit Hawaii. You always seem to know what to do to please me." She turned in his arms and slipped her hands around his neck. "Thank you, my love."

"The pleasure is all mine, believe me," he replied, just before his mouth found hers.

He could spend the rest of his life holding this woman, kissing her, making love to her...and that was exactly what he intended to do.

Without removing his mouth from hers, he picked her up and carried her to the bed, which was already turned back for them. Placing her in the middle, he found the hem of her gown and slowly raised it until he was forced to pause in his kiss so that he could lift it over her head.

The brilliant moonlight spotlit her where she lay, highlighting the peaks and curves, leaving provocative shadows to entice him to explore.

He sank down beside her, determined to make love to every inch of her body, from the tips of her toes all the way to the crown of her head.

By the time he had reached her knees she was shivering, her breath coming in small, shallow pants. He shifted so that he was lying between her knees as he continued his progress.

Her fingertips lightly caressed him, and he was reminded of fragile butterfly wings fluttering against his sensitive skin. He felt her tense as his lips followed an invisible path up her inner thigh. A muscle quivered, then was still.

He paused and raised his head. Her eyes sparkled in the moonlight. "With my body I thee worship," he said softly.

His next intimate kiss made her shift restlessly, but he relentlessly pursued her pleasure. Patiently he kissed and caressed her, until at last she cried out, her body rippling with the intensity of her reaction. Only then did he continue, still tracing an invisible path up her abdomen, her stomach and her breasts.

Once again he paused, teasing the tips with his flickering tongue until she moaned. His playfulness was having a strong effect on him, and he knew he could not prolong this much longer.

She took the choice away from him by blindly searching for his mouth as she boldly reached for his aroused masculinity. Lifting her hips to him and pulling him hard against her, she completed the union, holding him tightly.

They clung to each other, celebrating life. He began a steady pace that she matched. Slowly but inexorably he increased the intensity of the pace until the emotional storm they generated became a frenzy of passionate expression.

His cry echoed hers as they found the peak together, tumbling down the other side with whispered sighs and endearments. They were so much in tune with each other, each intuitively knowing and fulfilling the other's needs, wants, and desires. Unmeasured time drifted by as they lay there, still entwined, and watched the brilliant moon move across the heavens.

Sabrina kept her hand pressed lightly against his chest, enjoying the feel of his heart beating, of his lungs first filling with air, then releasing it. Her fingers traced the scars on his chest. Even after all this time she felt an ache whenever she remembered the time when she had almost lost him.

What a difference he had made in her life. She looked back on that poor woman who hadn't understood the fulfillment of a loving husband, a truly intimate relationship with someone who loved and accepted her, who made her feel so cherished.

"It seems almost impossible that we've been married five years," she said softly.

He stirred slightly and moved his hand lovingly across her hip. "In some ways, perhaps. Every time I make love to you I'm as excited as if it were the first time. And yet there are times when I can't remember what my life was like without you."

She placed a kiss on his jaw, wordlessly thanking him for his words.

"Are you sure Jessica has the number here?"

She grinned, though she knew he couldn't see it. "Yes, darling. She has our complete itinerary. She'll know where to contact us at any moment of our trip." She waited a moment. "Why do you ask?"

As if she didn't know.

"Oh, no reason in particular." He sounded very unconcerned. He didn't fool her a bit.

"I don't mind if you want to talk about them, you know. I miss them, too."

He lifted his head so that he could peer down into her moonlit face. Her warm smile and understanding expression made him feel more than a little sheepish. "It's just that they're so young, and we've never left them for this long before."

"I know. We discussed all of that before we left. But Michael, they're almost four years old. Besides, David and Diane have grown up with Jessica in their lives. She's like a second mother to them. In fact, she could be their mother."

He grinned. "I happen to know better. I remember the exact night they were conceived, not to mention being there when they made their entrance into our lives."

Sabrina remembered their conception quite well. Strip pool had become one of Michael's favorite forms of entertainment! She also remembered how wonderful he'd been to her all during her pregnancy, labor and delivery. He was there for them, all of them, whenever they needed him.

"Jessica was right, you know," he offered after several moments of silence. "Once she takes that job in New York, we won't have an opportunity to get away so easily."

"I know. I'm going to miss her."

"So will I. She's been a joy to be around."

"I wish that she and Steve got along better."

He looked down at her in surprise. "What do you mean? They seem to get along all right, don't they?"

"Well, with Steve's schedule he hasn't been home all that often, maybe twice when Jessica was home, but she always seems to change the subject whenever I bring him up."

"She's probably bored with listening to you rave on about him. To hear you talk about him, a person would think he walks on water."

Sabrina looked at him indignantly. "Well, I'm proud of him. Look what he's managed to accomplish in a few short years."

Michael nodded. "I know. He graduated with honors, got a job with a national television company and

is currently working out of their London news office."

"You have to admit he's done well."

"I do. I have. But I've also caught Jessica rolling
her eyes a couple of times when you start bragging
about him."

Sabrina laughed. "Really? Then maybe that's why
she changes the subject." She curled up against him.
"I'm glad to know it's not Steve, then."

"Why?" He wasn't sure he wanted to know the answer.

"Well, he's such a wonderful person. He'd make
any woman a marvelous husband."

"Sabrina! You know how much you hate match-
makers."

"I'm not matchmaking."

"What would you call it?"

"How could I matchmake with those two? They're
seldom home at the same time. They barely know each
other. He's in London, and she's going to be in New
York."

He groaned. "Knowing you, you'll come up with
some idea."

She smiled. "Let's just say that I'll enjoy watching
their careers progress. It's interesting that they're in
related fields."

"She's accepted a position writing for a travel
magazine, and he's a television news reporter. How
can that be related?"

"They're both in communications. Don't you see?"

He was quiet for a moment, but the hands moving across her body gave her a clue to what he was thinking.

"Sabrina?" he whispered.

"Hmmm?"

"I'm a great believer in communicating."

She smothered a chuckle. He certainly had a way of communicating his desires to her.

"Yes, Michael, I know."

There was no more need for words.

Jonathan and Daniel nodded to each other, shook hands and smiled, content with their success.

*   *   *   *   *

SILHOUETTE® *Desire*™

COMING NEXT MONTH

#553 HEAT WAVE—Jennifer Greene
Kat Bryant had always been cool to neighbor Mick Larson, but when she was forced to confront him about neglecting his motherless daughters sparks flew and the neighborhood really heated up!

#554 PRIVATE PRACTICE—Leslie Davis Guccione
Another Branigan-O'Connor union? According to Matthew Branigan and Bridget O'Connor—never! But when Bridget caught a glimpse of Matt's bedside manner, her knees got weak and her temperature started rising....

#555 MATCHMAKER, MATCHMAKER—Donna Carlisle
Old-fashioned chauvinist Shane Bartlett needed a wife and it was Cassie's job to find him one—an impossible task! But the search was surprisingly easy. These two opposites were the perfect match.

#556 MONTANA MAN—Jessica Barkley
He thought she was a spoiled socialite. She thought he was a jerk. Could Montana man Brock Jacoby ever tame a frisky filly like Jamaica McKenzie?

#557 THE PASSIONATE ACCOUNTANT—Sally Goldenbaum
Accountant Jane Barnett didn't like things she couldn't control—things like relationships—but Max Harris was proof that an emotional investment could yield a high return in love and happiness!

#558 RULE BREAKER—Barbara Boswell
Women never said no to rebel blue blood Rand Marshall, March's *Man of the Month*—but Jamie Saraceni did. One rejection from her and this rule breaker's bachelor days were numbered.

AVAILABLE NOW: